MURDER
IN THE
SHADOWS

BY

ELLEN GODFREY

CB

CONTEMPORARY BOOKS

a division of NTC/CONTEMPORARY PUBLISHING GROUP
Lincolnwood, Illinois USA

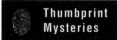
Thumbprint
Mysteries

MORE THUMBPRINT MYSTERIES

by Ellen Godfrey:

Murder on the Loose
Murder on the Lovers' Bridge

Special appreciation is due to Mary Elizabeth Devine, whose knowledge of Evanston proved indispensable.

This is a work of fiction. The characters, incidents, and dialogues are products of the author's imagination and are not to be construed as real. Any resemblance to actual events or persons, living or dead, is entirely coincidental.

Cover Illustration: David Lantz

ISBN: 0-8092-0686-2

Published by Contemporary Books,
a division of NTC/Contemporary Publishing Group, Inc.,
4255 West Touhy Avenue,
Lincolnwood (Chicago), Illinois 60646-1975 U.S.A.

90 QB 0 9 8 7 6 5 4 3 2 1

CHAPTER 1

No matter what anyone says, Tiffany Taylor is not a bimbo. Okay, she looks a little like one, with her blond hair cut in that punk style and the miniskirts, the big platform shoes, and all the makeup. But if you knew her the way I did, you'd know she's the kindest, gentlest person in the world. You would love her and want to protect her.

And, boy, does she need protection. Because the sad thing is, Tiffany Taylor is the kind of person that things happen to. I can't figure it out. She would never hurt a soul, yet she always seems to be in trouble—bad trouble, the kind of trouble that is catching. Hang around long enough with Tiffany and you're in trouble too. That's what happened to me.

To be fair, it's not that I need anyone to help me find trouble. I've found plenty on my own.

My name is Janet Barkin and I'm the one who started

the Women's Rescue Company. You may have seen us on TV because we solved two murders and made the six o'clock news both times. The second time was really big—we had a video of the bad guys trying to kill me and everyone saw me being brave in living color. For a moment there, I was famous and people thought I was a tough woman like I always dreamed they would.

The other women in the W.R.C.—Mrs. Gretzky, Porsha Moore, and Sally Lee—were famous too, but it didn't last. Don't they say everyone gets their fifteen minutes of fame and then poof—it's over? That's how it went with us. We took down a bunch of neighborhood bad guys and now here it is two months later and everyone's forgotten all about it. As far as people around here are concerned, we're just a bunch of neighborhood women with a storefront office who think we are big shots.

And who are we really? One overweight high school dropout—that's me. One old lady with bad legs—that's Mrs. Gretzky—and one pretty hairdresser with bad taste in men. That's my best friend, Sally. And one super-smart African-American teenager with big ambitions. That's Porsha.

Famous? Get real.

Still, even though I didn't feel like a famous, important person to myself, to Tiffany Taylor I was a hero.

Maybe that's where I went wrong. If I'd shown a little more humility, things might have turned out differently.

My ex-husband, Pat, is always telling me to face facts. He's always reminding me that I never finished high school and that I don't have a real job. He thinks I should let him protect me. I used to buy that line, but no longer. Now I stand up to him when he tries to bring me down—or I attempt to.

Anyway, I got caught up in Tiffany's troubles the day she

invited me to go with her on a picnic. Troubles? Is that the right word for the terrible events Tiffany was caught up in? I'll let you be the judge. Here's what happened.

*   *   *

"Lech!" Tiffany squealed the moment I opened the door to my apartment. She paid no attention to me but burst into the living room, dropped her basket on the floor, and flung herself upon my dog, hugging and kissing him. Lech licked her face and wagged his tail to show that he was glad to see her too.

"Oh, Lech, you darling, I've come to take you and Janet on the picnic like I promised!" Tiffany cried. "I brought, like, the *best* picnic lunch in the entire universe."

"It's good you came on Sunday," I said. "Lech hates to go out on Saturday morning and miss his cartoons."

Lech gave me a look that said, *watch it*. Lech doesn't like to be teased. He is a black German shepherd with an attitude. But he has a right to it because Lech is—quite simply—the best guard dog in the world, and I don't just say that because I love him so much.

I got him from my Polish landlady, Mrs. Gretzky. She named him Lech—pronounced "Lek"—after the Polish hero, Lech Walesa.

"You know what a hard time you gave me the time I made you miss '101 Dalmatians,'" I said to him.

Tiffany stood up and gave me a hug. "I'd never make Lech miss his cartoons," she said. "You should see what I have in the picnic basket. I got your favorite chocolate doughnuts, and I went to the Doggie Heaven store and bought the coolest stuff for Lech."

At this Lech perked up his ears, went over and sniffed the picnic basket, and wagged his tail happily.

"Sink let me borrow his 4X4 for the afternoon,"

Tiffany continued. "But I have to have it back by six, so come on, I'm double parked."

It was eleven o'clock on a dreary Sunday morning in October. As we came out of my apartment, I saw dark thunderclouds piling up toward the west. The air felt heavy and ominous and I looked at the sky. "I think it's going to rain," I said. "Maybe we should take some rain gear."

Tiffany frowned. "It can't rain. I've been planning this picnic *forever!* I'll never get Sink to loan me his 4X4 again. Lech needs to get out of the city and run and I promised him, didn't I, Lech?" She knelt down and ruffled Lech's fur. "Nothing's going to spoil our picnic."

A shiny red Jeep was parked outside my door with its top off. Tiffany opened the door and Lech jumped in. "Janet, do you mind driving?" Tiffany asked. "I mean, I'll drive if you want me to, but if anything happened to his Jeep, Sink would kill me."

"Sure. But I don't see Sink killing you," I said, climbing into the driver's seat. "Sink" was actually Alderman Gerry Synko, Tiffany's boss. Sink was a Big Man in the neighborhood, and we all loved him. If you got into trouble with the city government, or needed telephone or water fast, or had a kid picked up by the cops, all you had to do was call Sink and he'd straighten it out. Sink had a lot of powerful, important friends, but he never forgot the people he grew up with. When Tiffany dropped out of high school at seventeen, three years ago, and couldn't find a job, he gave her one in his office, although I could never exactly figure out what she did there.

"You're right, Sink wouldn't kill me," Tiffany said, handing me the car keys. "But Barbara would. For sure."

She sat back and strapped herself in as I started up the Jeep and pulled out into the traffic. Tiffany was wearing short cutoffs, huge black high-heeled sandals that must have weighed a ton, and a T-shirt that said "Blondes prefer Gentlemen." She had black lines pencilled around her eyes and black nail polish. I, on the other hand, was wearing an oversize Mickey Mouse T-shirt that covered up a lot that needed covering up. Plus wide-legged jeans, dirty sneakers, and a Chicago Cubs cap.

You'd never guess I'm practically a millionaire.

It's true. Last year I won $100,000 in the lottery, but it's a big secret and only my buddies in the Women's Rescue Company know. I used the lottery money to start the W.R.C. I don't spend it on myself, because I don't want people to know I won the lottery. I borrowed the money for the ticket and there are some people who would claim a share of my winnings if they knew.

"Why would Barbara kill you?" I asked.

Tiffany had been smiling happily but when she heard my question, a frightened look appeared on her face. "You know Barbara?" she said.

"She's Sink's executive assistant, right?"

"Right. She runs his office, she runs him, and she runs me too, I guess. I report to her and no matter what I do, she still hates me."

"Oh come on," I said. "I'm sure she doesn't hate you. She's probably under a lot of stress. Running an alderman's office has to be a tough job with everybody wanting stuff." At twenty, Tiffany was five years younger than me, but sometimes the age gap between us seemed much wider.

I pulled out onto Dempster Street and headed toward the tollway. There wasn't much traffic and I could see pale slivers of sun in the cracks in the clouds. Maybe it would clear up and we would have a nice picnic after all.

"Barbara does too hate me!" Tiffany said. "She thinks she is so perfect with her boring black suits and her briefcase and those stupid pumps she wears. She told me to take the ring out of my nose, but Sink said it didn't matter. Boy, was she mad when he stood up for me. I thought she would kill me right there."

There was something strange in Tiffany's voice when she said this. I glanced at her. She was staring out the window with a frightened look on her face.

It only took us half an hour to get to the forest preserve. We parked the Jeep, and Tiffany, Lech, and I set out walking along the path. Tiffany said she had a destination in mind. It was where their office had their Memorial Day picnic. There were picnic tables and an open field for Lech to explore.

"It's down this way," Tiffany told me.

She made good time in her high-heeled shoes with their big platforms. She looked neat in them, actually. You have to be thin to wear shoes like that. If I wore them, I'd look like an elephant on stilts.

Lech scampered along, running off the path into the forest from time to time to sniff at trees and weeds and bushes. He kept stopping to pee on things and I could tell he was having a great time. "How far is it?" I asked Tiffany.

"Through there," she said, pointing to a clearing ahead of us.

We came out into a picnic place. There was a stone barbecue, some picnic tables, a trash can, and a small grassy patch that sloped down toward the lagoon. It probably looked real pretty on a sunny day, but in the gloom, it seemed kind of depressing. There was no one there but us. Bits of trash lay about and there were empty beer cans on both tables.

"Isn't this great!" Tiffany said, spreading her arms. "We

had such a good time here this summer. Sink was soooo nice to me. Barbara practically had a hissy fit right there!" She pointed to one of the tables.

"Sounds like maybe you have a thing for Sink," I said. "Isn't he old? About fifty? And married?"

Tiffany hung her head. "I know," she said. "You're right, I'm an idiot, I know that. Hey! Where's Lech?"

"Lech!" I called. "Lech!"

Suddenly I heard a howl that made my blood run cold. I knew that sound and I knew what it meant.

"Lech!" I commanded. "Here! Now!"

A minute later Lech came leaping into the clearing from the woods. His fur was puffed up around his neck and his ears and tail were rigid. He ran up to me, then turned and ran back the way he had come.

I went after him.

"Janet!" Tiffany called. I ignored her. I followed Lech into the woods.

I ran after Lech, just keeping him in sight. He streaked through the woods, between the trees, turning from time to time to be sure I was following.

It was dark in there, but the trees were far apart and the ground was spongy underfoot, so it was easy to run after Lech. I could hear Tiffany stumbling along after me in her high heels. "Janet! Where are you going? Come back here! Hey!"

I caught up with Lech to find him standing over something, his fur bristling. He gave that terrible howl again.

I looked down.

A woman lay sprawled among the rotting leaves and crushed ferns. She wore a black suit, white silk shirt, and black pumps. Beside one outstretched hand lay a briefcase—open, empty.

Beside her a great knobby branch, fallen from a dead tree, lay across the path. The branch was stained with dark blood.

I knew at once she was dead. Anyone would have known it because her head had been bashed to a bloody pulp and her face was completely gone. Around her head, the leaves and dirt were covered with black dried blood.

"Oh my God," I said, the words catching in my throat.

Tiffany came up behind me. "Hey, Janet! What are you—"

She stopped short, saw what I was looking at, and screamed, "It's Barbara! It's Barbara! Holy Mother of God!"

I turned to Tiffany and saw that all the color had drained out of her face. I had never seen anyone so white in my life. Her makeup stood out on her skin, so she looked like a terrified clown with blotches of red on her cheeks. She stretched out a hand and grabbed at me, her legs wobbling. I held onto her and I could hear her breath gasping in her throat.

I led her slowly back to the picnic clearing. "Calm down, calm down, you're okay," I said to her gently. I sat her down on the picnic bench.

"I think I'm going to faint," Tiffany whispered.

"Put your head down between your knees," I said. I opened the basket and took out a can of Coke, found a plastic cup, filled it, and handed it to her.

She drank it, making a face. "Ugh. It's warm. I meant to put the cans in the lagoon to get cool."

"Never mind about that. Drink it."

She swallowed some more.

"Are you feeling better?" I asked, sitting down beside her.

Lech came up to her and put his nose on her lap. He was checking to be sure she was okay too. She gave him a weak smile and patted him.

"I'm okay now." But tears had begun to run down her face. "I can't believe it," she said. "Barbara. I can't believe it. Who would have done that to her? How could I have said those mean things about her? Oh, I feel sick!"

"How do you know it's Barbara?" I asked. "Her face—"

"Don't say it! Don't say it!" Tiffany cried. "I'll never forget how she looked. Of course it's Barbara! I know that suit. I know that blouse. I know that ring. I know the briefcase and I know those stupid black pumps with the dorky heels and those dinky little gold earrings. Who could have done that to her? Why?"

She had seen a lot for one quick glance. "Yes," I said. "And what was she doing out here dressed for a business meeting?" I opened my purse, took out my cell phone, and dialed 911.

CHAPTER 2

"Accident?" cried Tiffany, dabbing at her tear-filled eyes with a tissue. "Barbara killed by accident? No way!"

We were sitting around the office of the Women's Rescue Company. Tiffany, Mrs. Gretzky, Sally, Porsha, and me. And Lech, of course, who was curled up under my desk, licking his paws and looking depressed. I didn't blame him because I wasn't feeling great either. I kept seeing in my mind's eye Barbara Noyes' smashed-up face lying among bloody leaves and weeds.

It hadn't helped that after reporting to the police and answering questions for what seemed like hours, Tiffany and I had failed to convince them that Barbara had been murdered. They claimed it was "too soon to make that determination." Whatever that meant.

I know cops. I shouldn't have been surprised by the way they acted, but I was. My ex-husband, Pat Barkin, is a cop. He's an undercover cop, and you can't believe half the stuff they tell you. They deceive people as part of their job, and it gets to be a habit.

I'd called Pat the next morning, after the discovery of Barbara's body and after we gave our statements to the police.

The first thing Pat said when he heard my voice was, "What do *you* want?"

"Come on, Pat," I said. "Don't be that way."

"Whadya mean, don't be that way? You tell me not to call you. You never call me. Then all of a sudden, out of the blue, you call. I bet you want some kind of favor."

"That's not fair."

"Fair? You probably want to know about Barbara Noyes. Am I right or am I right?"

"You're right," I admitted.

"Why didn't you call your new friend Larry? From what I hear you have him dancing on the end of your string."

This hurt. After Pat and I broke up, for a long time I felt so low and ugly and stupid I thought no man would ever be interested in me. Then I met Larry Keegan. He is a detective in the police and a lot higher up than Pat. More important, he is kind and he treats me like an equal. Larry is truly special, and for a while it looked like something wonderful was going to happen between us.

But I must have screwed up, because lately he hasn't been coming around. I'd called him before I called Pat, and he hadn't returned my call. I hated to admit it, but it seemed like Larry was avoiding me. That's why I'd been reduced to calling Pat, and he had every right to be annoyed. But still, I wanted to know what the police thought about Barbara Noyes' death, so I had to take what he dished out.

"I thought you'd know," I said in my sweetest voice. "You hear everything."

"I do, that's true," Pat said. "Not much goes on in this neighborhood I don't know about."

"All my friends told me if you want to know what's really going on, ask Pat," I said, laying it on so thick I thought he might see through me.

But he didn't because he said in a boastful tone, "My eyes are everywhere, know what I mean?"

"So how did she die?" I asked.

"Barbara Noyes? Too soon to say. Her case is still open. But off the record, it looks like they're going to call it an accident."

"What? How can that be?"

"Easy. Sink wants it to be an accident. He says everybody loved her and nobody'd have a reason to kill her. Nobody benefits from her death. Looks like the branch of a dead tree just fell on her. Her bad luck that she was in the wrong place at the wrong time, that's all there is to it."

"I don't believe this," I said.

"Believe it."

"Just because Sink wants it to be an accident, that's it?" I asked, incredulous.

"That's it, babe. You didn't hear it from me, though. Say, I can't hang around chatting all day. Gotta run."

I hung up the phone, stunned. How could the police be so stupid? So blind?

And now, here I was, sitting at the W.R.C. office, telling my friends what I'd found out and they were reacting exactly as I had.

"She was wearing a business suit, shoes with skinny little high heels, and carrying her briefcase!" Tiffany said.

"Do the police really think a woman goes for a walk in the woods in that outfit?" Sally asked me.

I shook my head.

"She was there to meet someone, had to be," Porsha chimed in. "They had an argument, he lured her off the path, picked up the branch, and beat her upside the head. That's what you said it looked like, right?"

"Right."

"Men. They can be *so* stupid about some things," Porsha said.

Porsha was just finding out the facts of life. She was seventeen and the smartest person I knew. She went to a Catholic girls' school where she got straight A's and won all the prizes. She was totally focused on doing well and making a success out of her life. Porsha wants to be a lawyer and I have no doubt she will make it. Colleges are already scouting her.

She was cool and pretty too, with her skin the color of a shiny new penny. She wore her hair pulled back and tied in a knot of skinny braids, decorated with colored beads. But with her studies, helping around the house because her mama worked two jobs, and helping us at the W.R.C., she didn't have too much time for men.

Tiffany nodded. "Read my T-shirt," she said. "It says it all."

Tiffany was wearing a leather miniskirt, tall boots with huge, heavy high heels and inch-thick platform soles. She had on a T-shirt with a frog on the front. Under the frog it said: "You need to kiss a lot of frogs to get your prince." The frog was green and Tiffany wore nail polish to match.

Mrs. Gretzky said, "So. This Barbara Noyes? I met her one time."

We all turned to look at Mrs. Gretzky. She looked good. She'd just been to Hair-Today, the beauty shop where Sally works. Sally had given her a new perm, so her scalp didn't show through the gray hairs like it usually did. Instead of the cotton housedress and slippers she normally wears, she had on a powder-blue dress and a fuzzy, gray sweater. Mrs. Gretzky has seen a lot in her seventy-eight years. You just look at her and you know she is wise.

"How did that happen?" I asked her. "You meeting Barbara, I mean."

"I went to see Alderman Synko to ask him to help my nephew, Stanislaus," Mrs. Gretzky said.

Mrs. Gretzky's nephew is always in some kind of trouble.

"Did Sink help?" I asked.

"That Barbara sits at a desk out in the front like she's the big shot," Mrs. Gretzky said. "She wouldn't let me talk to the alderman. She just wrote down everything I said and acted like a queen."

"You didn't like her?"

Mrs. Gretzky considered. "I got to be fair here," she said. "I told her Stan lost his job and needed to find something and a week later she called and said Alderman Synko found him a job with Bauer Construction. Turned out, it was a good job too."

"I thought those were all union jobs," Porsha said.

"They are," Mrs. Gretzky said. "But Alderman Synko took care of it. So I guess I shouldn't say anything against her."

"I shouldn't have either," Tiffany sniffled, tears welling up in her eyes. "I can't believe I was saying bad things about her when she was lying there all beat-up in her own blood."

"Oh, don't start crying again, honey," Sally said. She came around and put her arms around Tiffany and hugged her. "It's not your fault."

"I know," sobbed Tiffany, "but it feels like it is because I talked so mean behind her back. We've got to find out who killed her. Sink won't know what to do without her. Barbara ran that office and told everyone what to do and where to go." She jumped up. "Heavens, what am I doing here? I should be at the office, helping Sink. I'm a stupid idiot. A total, stupid idiot!"

"Don't be so hard on yourself," Porsha said. "You've had a terrible shock."

"Janet," Tiffany said, "will you come to the ward office with me? Will you tell Sink that we have to find out who murdered Barbara? We can't let the police go on thinking it was an accident. Somebody did this to her. They can't get away with it. It's not right!"

"I don't know . . ." I began. I hadn't told Tiffany it was because of Sink that the police were calling Barbara's death an accident. Sink was a powerful, respected man. People listened to him and no one wanted to go against him. Why would they? He was always on our side.

"You've got to!" Tiffany said. "And the W.R.C. has to solve the case like you did those other murders."

"Wait a minute," I said.

"I think that's a real good idea," Porsha said.

"This a job for the police, not us. We help women," I said. "We can't help Barbara. It's too late for that."

"I can't believe you said that!" Tiffany cried. "Aren't you a big hero? You're going to let a neighborhood woman be beaten to a pulp and sit there and do nothing? You're supposed to be brave and stand up for women."

"That's not fair," I said.

Tiffany was at the door. "What do you think, Lech?" she said. "You're not going to lie back and take it, are you? Don't *you* want to get whoever did that to Barbara?"

Lech got up and trotted toward the door. Then he turned and they both looked at me.

"Come on, Janet," Tiffany said.

"Looks like you're outnumbered," Porsha observed.

*   *   *

You could tell as soon as you opened the door to Sink's headquarters that something bad had happened. Phones were ringing and no one was answering. People were hanging around, not doing anything, looking confused. A man caught sight of Tiffany and shouted, "Tiffany! There you are. For God's sake, take the phones, will you?"

"Sorry, sorry," Tiffany said. She scooted over to a desk, sat down, and picked up a ringing phone. "Hello? Alderman Synko's headquarters. How may I help you?" she said.

The man who had scolded her was a tall, bearded guy in jeans. "Take messages," he said. "Sink's not talking to anyone today. Give the messages to me. I'll handle them for now. God. Everything's falling apart around here."

"Can you hold a minute?" Tiffany said into the phone. She pressed a button and said, "Hello? Alderman Synko's headquarters. How may I help you? Can you hold a minute?" She pressed another button. "Hello? Alderman Synko's . . ."

The door in the back of the room flew open. Out popped Alderman Synko. He was a giant of a man, six-foot-four, over three hundred pounds, with a round red face topped by a few scraggly blond hairs. He wore gray suit pants and bright red suspenders over a white dress

shirt that stretched over his huge belly. He took one look
at me and cried, "Janet! Janet Barkin! What a terrible
thing for you!"

He rushed over to me and flung his arms around me,
squeezing me to him in a giant bear hug. Then he pulled
back and looked at me. "Janet! You gorgeous thing! Why
do we have to meet again on such a sad occasion! It takes
a tragedy to get you to come around? Is that fair? Don't
you know you're my kind of woman? When are you
going to make me happy? Look at you! All woman and
every inch delicious! Hey, your hair! What have you
done to it!"

I couldn't believe he remembered I used to wear my
hair long. I'd only seen Sink once or twice over the last
few years at neighborhood barbecues, along with about a
zillion other people. He'd shaken my hand, given me a
compliment, then moved on to do the same to the next
person. But I guess politicians are good at remembering
details and flattering people.

"Sally cut my hair short and now I'm letting it grow
out. I know it doesn't look . . ."

"It's sexy. I love it. When are you going to make me
happy?"

"Not today," I said.

He put his hand on my arm and caressed it gently. His
hand was very pink and the back was covered with heavy
yellow hair. "You're breaking my heart," he said, looking
sadly into my eyes. Then his expression changed. "You've
come about Barbara, of course," he said. "I know you and
Tiffany found her body. Come on into my office. We
need to talk."

Sink took my arm and led me into his office. He sat
me down on a chair and patted my shoulder several

times, brushing up against me as he did so. Then he went around behind his desk, sat down with a big sigh, and smoothed his hands over his face.

"So how've you been, Janet?" Sink said. "You sure have turned into a beautiful woman. I remember you when."

I didn't know what he was talking about. I stared at him. Sink had a round red face with twinkling blue eyes and smile lines raying out from his eyes, a double chin, and the swollen red nose of man who drinks too much. There was something about Sink's face, about his easy smile, that made you want to smile too. You felt whatever the problem, Sink would just laugh and then fix it.

"You don't remember how I used to tease you?" he asked, pretending to be hurt. "That was when I hung around with your brother, Dennis, when you were a little sprout. I can't believe I didn't make more of an impression on you. After all, I was better looking then." He picked up a pencil from his desk, stuck it down the front of his shirt, and scratched his chest with it.

"Dennis?" I said. "You were a friend of Dennis's?" My brother Dennis is twelve years older than me. Dennis has worked hard. He went to law school at night and got a degree and is making good money as a lawyer. Although I admire what he has accomplished, we don't get along very well and I hardly ever see him.

"Hey," I said. It was coming back to me. "Weren't you and Dennis law partners a long time ago?"

"That's right," Sink said. "You must have been a little girl then. Dennis and me, we both graduated law school at the same time and opened a law office together. But then he went off on his own, I went into politics, and as they say, the rest is history."

"I remember now," I said. "Wasn't Dennis real mad at you? Are you guys still friends?"

"Of course we're still friends! You know Dennis. He'd like to stay mad, but I don't let people stay mad at me. Never let the sun go down on your anger, that's my motto."

Sink was right about my brother because Dennis was a great one for holding a grudge. It was easy to insult him without meaning to or even knowing you had. And if you did, that was it and he turned against you. That's what had happened between Dennis and me.

"I wish I knew how you could stay friends with Dennis," I admitted. "I can't pull it off."

"He didn't send you, then?" Sink asked.

"Send me? Dennis? I haven't talked to him in a couple of years. The last time I saw him was at my grandpa's funeral. No. Tiffany and I wanted to talk to you about Barbara."

Sink shook his head. "What a tragedy. What a terrible, terrible thing. She was a wonderful woman. Brilliant organizer. Invaluable. One in a million."

But I was still puzzling over why Sink would think Dennis had sent me. "About Dennis . . ."

"No, I don't hold it against him. Or her, for that matter. But surely," here Sink leaned forward over his desk, his twinkling blue eyes looking into mine, "he's going to have to drop the lawsuit now. With Barbara dead and all."

"What suit?" I asked.

"You didn't know?"

I shook my head.

"Just a misunderstanding. A simple misunderstanding. She wouldn't have gone through with it. I'm sure of that. We were friends."

"I'm sorry," I said. "I don't know what you're talking about."

Sink leaned even farther over his desk toward me. "Barbara was suing me."

I couldn't believe it. "How come? Didn't she work for you?" I had never heard of anyone suing their boss before. At least, not while they still worked for the boss.

"Yes," Sink said. "And she went on working for me, even after they filed suit, doing a great job. She ran this office like clockwork. I don't know what we're going to do without her. Did you see them out there, running around like chickens with their heads cut off?"

"But what did she sue you for?"

Sink smiled. "It's the craziest thing in the world. She sued me for sexual harassment. I told her it was a misunderstanding. You know me, I love women. That's my way. I want to make love to every pretty woman I see. Of course, I prefer big, round, juicy women. Like you." He stopped for a minute and looked me up and down admiringly. "But Barbara was a lovely thing and I told her so. She would just laugh and joke about it. She never took it the wrong way."

"Well then, why did she sue?" I asked.

Sink's smile vanished. He looked sad. "I don't know. I hate to say this to you, but I think it was your brother, Dennis. He put her up to it."

"Why would he do that?" I asked.

"That's Dennis," Sink said.

"I'm sorry, I don't get it."

"Dennis holds grudges. He always has. In high school, we played football together. We were the two best guys on the team. After his injury, after his knee got smashed up, I went on to be a big star and of course, he was off the team and he blamed me. It was crazy, but he did. Later we started our law practice together. The only business we could get, two guys with law degrees from night school, was crooks. Defending crooks. Now, don't get me wrong," Sink raised his hand, "crooks need a defense. I know that."

"I guess they do," I said doubtfully.

"Of course they do!" Sink said. "It was your brother who taught me that. He told me our justice system depends on it and you can make money doing it too. But one day I realized I couldn't take it anymore. So I said to him, 'Well, everyone deserves his day in court. But when I start wanting our clients to lose, it's time to move on. I'm going into politics where I can do some good instead of helping bad guys do bad.'"

"How did Dennis take that?" I asked.

"Not well," Sink said. "He thought I let him down by leaving the partnership we had started together. After I won the election, got to be alderman, I tried to make it up to him. And he acted like we were friends again, but well, as I said, you know Dennis."

"Dennis can hide his feelings when he wants to," I agreed.

"He'll smile and act friendly," Sink said, "but in his heart, he is planning revenge. You know his favorite expression? 'Revenge is a dish best eaten cold.'"

"Yes," I said sadly. I had heard Dennis say this when talking about some enemy of his. The expression had always made me shiver.

"So I guess I wasn't too surprised when he talked Barbara into suing me for sexual harassment," Sink said. "But I knew the lawsuit would never get to court. If I had to settle, I would have. Dennis and I had a meeting set up for tomorrow. I told him I wanted to talk settlement. Of course, what they said about me wasn't true, I never harassed anybody. But a sexual harassment charge wouldn't look good if it got in the papers. So far, we've kept the whole thing low profile. I figured the best thing was to get the problem behind us. Settle. Pay whatever Barbara thought was fair."

"But now Barbara's dead," I reminded him.

"Yes. But I'm still kind of worried. That's why I was so glad to see you this morning. Could you talk to Dennis for me? See if he's willing to drop the whole thing?"

"Why wouldn't he drop it?" I asked. "If Barbara's dead, it's over, right?"

"Any other lawyer, that'd be right," Sink said. "But your brother, I'm afraid this was kind of a grudge match for him. I'm worried he'll spread rumors about me—stories that could hurt me. Make things sound worse than they were."

"So that's it!" I said.

"What do you mean?" Sink asked, looking puzzled.

"That's why you don't want Barbara's death to be murder. You're afraid the story about the sexual harassment suit will get out if there's a murder investigation."

Sink looked at me and smiled as if I had cracked a joke. "This sexual harassment business hit me out of left field. If I did something that upset someone, why not just tell me?"

I didn't say anything.

"I know I'm a flirt," he said. "Maybe sometimes I go too far. But you don't mind, do you, Janet? How could you mind if I think you're beautiful and I tell you so?"

"Yes, I do mind," I said.

His face fell and for a moment he looked as if he were going to cry. Then he brightened up. "You don't like it even a little bit?" he said. "To know that someone's admiring those curves of yours?"

He looked like a pathetic puppy. The way he tilted his head to one side and smiled hopefully at me, I couldn't stop myself from smiling back at him. You couldn't stay mad at Sink.

"Let's be serious, Sink," I said. "Barbara's dead. Someone murdered her. We can't just pretend it never happened."

"It never happened," Sink said. "It was an accident. That's what will be best for me and best for Dennis and best for the neighborhood. Trust me."

CHAPTER 3

I left Tiffany hard at work pressing buttons on the phone and telling everyone to hold, and walked back to the W.R.C. office. I thought over my conversation with Alderman Synko and I felt very uneasy. The sky was dark and the air still. It seemed quiet somehow, even though traffic rushed by me, horns honked, and sirens wailed—all the usual noise of a busy street in Evanston, Illinois, on a weekday morning. I felt as if a storm might be brewing off to the west, maybe even a tornado.

As Lech and I walked, I thought about my brother Dennis. I should go see him and find out what he had been up to with Barbara Noyes. I realized I was rubbing my arm where Sink had caressed it, as if I was trying to rub away his touch. It had felt creepy somehow.

I walked past a cafe and looked inside, thinking I might go in for a cup of coffee.

My heart went bang in my chest. Larry was there, sitting at a table near the window, having coffee with a pretty woman. She sat sideways to the window, and I could see that she was about my age. She wore a sweatshirt and jeans. Her blond hair was twisted into a braid that went down her back and a few wavy blond hairs hung loose around her face. Larry was talking seriously to her and she was shaking her head as if she didn't agree with what he was saying.

Right away I thought the worst, that this pretty woman proved Larry was avoiding me. She was his new love. He hadn't been working hard like he told me the few times I caught up with him; he'd been with *her*. And why not? Even from where I was standing, I could see her flat stomach, her tight jeans. The way she sat, so tall and fit looking, she probably lifted weights and jogged. How could I compete with someone like that?

How handsome Larry looked with his wavy brown hair, his strong chin, and the way his shirt pulled over the muscles in his back. Suddenly, I wanted a cigarette. I hadn't had one in over nine months, but I wanted one badly.

Lech was looking in the window too. The door to the coffee shop opened and someone came out. Lech dashed in and trotted over to Larry. I watched, rooted to the spot, as Larry caught sight of Lech, then looked up and saw me. I wanted to disappear. I needed a blackout, like on TV, but none came.

Larry said something to the woman. Then he stood, patted Lech, and the two of them—Larry and Lech— came out onto the sidewalk. "Janet!" Larry said. "I've been meaning to call you."

"That's okay," I said weakly, not looking at him. "I've been busy too."

"No, really," Larry said. "It's this case I'm on; it's taking up all my time."

I looked in the window at the blond. Then I looked back at him. I could see how uncomfortable he was, how he couldn't meet my eyes. "Sure," I said. "Don't worry about it. I was just passing by on my way back from visiting Alderman Synko."

"Sink?" Larry said sharply. "Why were you visiting him?"

"Tiffany Taylor asked me to," I said. "Anyway, I'm in a hurry. See you around."

He took my hand. I let it lie limply in his. "Janet, I miss you. I want to see you. As soon as I can, I will. Trust me on this, Janet, I'll explain everything, I promise."

"Yeah," I said. "Okay. Whatever. Come on, Lech, we have to go talk to Dennis."

I pulled my hand away and started to walk down the street. "Janet!" Larry called after me, but I didn't turn around and I pretended not to hear him. *"Janet!"* He called again, but I ignored him and kept on going.

That was the second time in an hour a man had said "trust me." And I didn't trust either of them.

*   *   *

I called Dennis's office on my cell phone and they told me he was at home, so I dropped Lech off at my apartment and took the Metra train out to where Dennis lived. The tracks run parallel to the lake, a few blocks to the west. When I got off at the station, I could see the dark, heavy layer of clouds boiling over Lake Michigan. The air felt even heavier out here in the 'burbs, and looking toward the lake, I saw flashes of lightning. I heard the rumble of thunder, very faint, in the distance.

Dennis lived in a condo near the village of Hubbard

Woods. I walked to his place, trying not to think about Larry and his new blond girlfriend. If he wanted to dump me, why didn't he just do it? Why did he say he was going to call and not follow through? I hate that. You wait and wait for a phone call that never comes and having a cell phone makes it worse. You're waiting for that call every minute of the day. Why did he say he wanted to see me and then act so weird? If the blond girl was just a friend, wouldn't he have offered to introduce me?

It turned out Dennis was not that thrilled to see me either.

"Oh, it's you," he said when he opened the front door.

"Yes, it's me. Your very own sister."

Dennis just stood there, leaning on his cane and looking at me as if he'd never seen me before in his life. My brother was almost as tall as Sink, but he wasn't fat. While Sink had ballooned up in the years since they were high school football champs, my brother had shriveled. He was thirty-seven but he looked older. The bones in his cheeks stood out, and his eyes had dark patches under them like bruises. There were deep frown lines between his eyes, and his brown hair had started to go gray around his ears. "Well, as long as you're here, I guess you better come in," he said finally.

He turned and limped away from me, tapping his cane angrily on the floor as he walked.

I followed him to a neat living-dining room where piles of file folders were stacked on the dining room table. Dennis gestured to a chair and I sat down.

"Where's Red?" I asked. Like me, Dennis loves dogs. Our dad taught us how to train dogs and we both were good at it. Red was an old Irish setter who had been

Dennis's best friend for years.

"He died," Dennis said. "About five months ago."

"Oh," I said. "I didn't know. I'm sorry."

"Cut the crap, Janet. You don't care about my dog. Why are you here?"

I felt like asking what had I ever done to him that he would talk to me like that, but the truth is, all the men in my family are rude to women—unless the women are very important. That's just how they are and they'll never change.

"I was talking to Alderman Synko, and he told me you and Barbara were suing him."

"Damn right. He's a dirty old man and we could prove it. Barbara documented every unwanted pass, every suggestive statement and gesture, and she has it all on file."

"Wow," I said, thinking of all the suggestive things Sink had said to me in only a half hour. "That must be a pretty thick file."

Dennis balled his hand into a fist and shook it at me. "We had him. He would have had to pay off big-time, and then she had to go and get brained by a dead tree branch. I came this close," he held his thumb and forefinger an inch apart, "to the Big Score. Sink has the luck of the Irish all right, except he's not Irish and I am. Go figure." He almost smiled, and for an instant I thought I saw the old Dennis, the brother I used to be close to before he smashed his knee on the football field and changed to the person he is now, a person I can't get along with.

Dennis sat down in a chair opposite me, laying his cane carefully next to the chair so he could use it to get up. "Did he send you to make an offer?" he asked.

"Make an offer?" I said. "Why would he do that? Barbara's dead. You'll have to drop the suit now, right?"

Dennis studied me. "I don't get it. What are you up to? Why did you come out here?"

"Dennis," I said, "Barbara didn't die in an accident. I was there and I saw her body. Somebody bashed her head in."

Dennis face got bright red. "No! You're out of your mind!"

"It's true."

Dennis looked down at his hands. They were pressed onto his knees so hard the knuckles were white. As I watched, the flush faded from his face and he slumped lower in the chair. "Did you know her?" he asked softly.

"I never met her," I replied. "But my friend Tiffany worked with her and she told me all about her."

"Barbara was a wonderful woman," Dennis said. "Smart, pretty, organized. She had character. Remember, Dad used to say that about people? When he really looked up to someone, he'd say the person had character?"

"Yes. It was his biggest compliment."

"She was proud of her high standards," Dennis continued. "She was proud of working for Alderman Synko because he cared for ordinary working people and tried so hard to see that they got a fair shake. She said everyone was always trying to take advantage of his good nature, and she saw her job as protecting him from himself."

Dennis was talking quietly, not looking at me. I wondered if he had been in love with Barbara, because I had never heard him talk about a woman like this. Dennis was divorced—no kids. I didn't know much about his love life since he and his wife had parted.

"So if she felt like that, why did she sue him?" I asked.

"She had tried every way she could to get him to act respectful toward women. She tried and tried to tell him that times had changed."

I thought to myself that Dennis had never got it, so why would he expect Sink to. But I didn't say anything.

"Nothing worked," Dennis went on. "She felt she owed it to the other women in the office—to your friend Tiffany, to the volunteers, to the women voters who came to ask for favors. Sink came on to everyone and some women thought they needed to give in if they wanted his help. She tried to explain to him how women felt about the way he acted, but he couldn't see it. Barbara didn't want to go to court, she didn't want a big settlement, she just wanted him to change."

"Do you think he would have?" I asked.

"Barbara thought so. We were claiming big money in damages, but we didn't really mean to push it to that point. We expected to negotiate, settle for something that hurt, but not too bad, and for a document that would hold his feet to the fire."

"Feet to the fire?"

"We were going to hold out until he signed a consent decree, until he put it in writing that he would clean up his act. And if he didn't, he'd have to pay out more."

"Sink's afraid of the bad publicity," I said.

"I know. That was our ace in the hole," Dennis said. "That's why I thought he sent you. To talk me out of going to the newspapers. He's afraid the story will get out now that she's gone. He knew she cared about him and I don't. He's afraid I'm after revenge because of the way he screwed me over our law practice. And some other old scores between us."

"Is that what you want—revenge?" I asked.

"Sink isn't the saint everyone thinks he is, you know that?" Dennis said.

I didn't reply.

"You think I'm just saying that because I hate him." Dennis flashed that old familiar smile. "Well, maybe you're right. But it's still true."

"About Barbara's death," I began.

Dennis shook his head. "Let her rest in peace, Janet," he said. "Don't get all emotional over a terrible accident. Accept it. It's fate."

"I can't accept it," I said. "Fate didn't swing that branch."

"Look. I know you solved some murders. So now probably you see murderers everywhere. You've been on TV twice. Isn't that enough for you? It's sick, trying to use a terrible accident to get publicity for yourself. Do you think Alderman Synko will pay you off or donate to your stupid women's center if you push him into a corner? Forget about it."

That's how Dennis's mind worked. He was always looking for an angle and he thought everyone else was too. I couldn't help but think that this nasty crack was more like him than all the nice things he'd said about Barbara.

I stood up. "You can't talk to me like that anymore," I said. "I'm leaving. But here's one thing you'd better face up to. Barbara Noyes was murdered. And me and the Women's Rescue Company, we're going to find out who did it."

CHAPTER
4

"It's a cover-up. That's the only explanation," Porsha said.

"Check the cabbage rolls, will you?" Mrs. Gretzky said to Sally. "They shouldn't simmer too hard."

We were in Mrs. Gretzky's kitchen helping her fix dinner. It was Tuesday evening, the day after I had talked to Sink and Dennis. We needed to figure out what to do next and Mrs. Gretzky had invited us over to her apartment for dinner and a planning session.

Mrs. Gretzky stood at the stove, wearing her usual cotton housedress and a big apron. Her knee-high stockings were rolled down around her ankles and her legs looked swollen and painful. Sally, who was the best cook after Mrs. Gretzky, had offered to make the dinner, but Mrs. Gretzky wouldn't hear of it.

So Sally moved around the kitchen helping. She looked as beautiful as always, her blond hair curled and held up with a big purple plastic comb and her makeup as perfect as a TV star's. Sally is an expert on hair and nails and makeup. She earns the most in tips of anyone at her beauty salon, and rich ladies drive in from Winnetka and Glencoe just to have Sally do their hair.

Porsha sat at the kitchen table, mashing potatoes. Mrs. Gretzky had taken the pot off the stove and handed it to Porsha, along with a masher and pitcher of milk and a knob of butter.

Lech was under the table, but everytime Sally lifted the lid of the cabbage-roll pot, he stuck his nose out hopefully. I felt too antsy to sit. I stood, leaning my back against the window. The kitchen was steamy and smelled of cabbage rolls and freshly baked Polish cornbread and apple strudel.

These were the women of the W.R.C. The women who—along with me—had solved two murders and helped many neighborhood women in trouble. If anyone could figure out what was going on, they could.

"What do you mean, cover-up?" Sally asked Porsha.

"Like I said, no woman goes walking in the woods in a business suit. Then she goes off the path carrying her briefcase? Ends up dead and the two men she works closest with want it to be an accident? Won't hear tell that it might be murder? It doesn't compute." Porsha gave the potatoes a specially hard mash and poured in a little milk. She added a chunk of butter, picked up a wooden spoon, and started to stir.

"Mark my words and write it in a book," Mrs. Gretzky said, opening the refrigerator and taking out a jar of pickles. "There are secrets being hidden. Something that won't look good for Alderman Synko if it gets out. That Barbara woman went here and there and everywhere. Mixing herself up in everybody's business, acting like she knew best."

"That was her job," I said. "Anyway, I told you, I found out the secret. Barbara was suing Sink for sexual harassment. How big a secret can that be anyway? When you sue someone, it gets around."

"What's this sexual harassment?" Mrs. Gretzky said. "Men with bad manners have been giving women trouble since Adam and Eve. It's against the law now? Is it supposed to be that we ladies are too dumb to open our mouths and tell a man to behave himself?"

Mrs. Gretzky had seen a lot of life, but she had never been what you might call a working woman. She'd seen war and death in Poland as a young girl. She'd come to America with her husband. Together they ran a plumbing business. He did the plumbing work and she kept the books.

Now Mr. Gretzky was dead and Mrs. Gretzky had turned her house into a three-plex. I lived on the top story, Porsha and her mama lived on the ground floor, and Mrs. Gretzky had the basement apartment. Mrs. Gretzky kept the books for the W.R.C. and did a great job. She did all the paperwork for the government too. But I don't think she understood how it felt to need a paycheck and have a male boss who made your skin creep.

"It doesn't do any good to tell Sink to behave himself," I said. "He thinks he's giving you a compliment when he talks about your body and rubs up against you."

"Big deal," Mrs. Gretzky snorted. She opened the pickle jar and began putting pickles into a dish. "That should be the worst thing that ever happens to you in life."

"It's horrible to have to put up with a man touching you and saying things. It's awful to be afraid that if you try and stop it, you'll lose your job," Sally said with a shiver. "I did the models' hair stylings for a photo shoot once. The producer had his hands all over the models. It was disgusting, but they were afraid to say anything. One was only fourteen, and I saw her crying when no one was looking. That guy was a real slimebucket and no one stopped him."

"So did you say anything?" Porsha asked.

Sally looked down. "I was afraid to," she admitted. "Everyone wants to do fashion shoots, and I didn't want to blow my chances. But he must have seen how disgusted I looked, because even though my stylings got heaps of compliments, that producer never asked me back."

Mrs. Gretzky shrugged. "Well, rape, making a woman do things, that I call harassment. But this other nonsense?" She handed me the bowl of pickles to take into the living room where her dining table was. It looked so pretty with silverware, fancy plates, and real cloth napkins. At my place, I ate leaning over the sink or at the kitchen table.

Mrs. Gretzky heaped our plates with cabbage rolls, Polish cornbread, and mashed potatoes. Sally and Porsha carried the plates into the living room. I put a cabbage roll and potatoes in a tin pie plate for Lech. At my house he mostly gets dog food, so this was his lucky day. Of course, he does prefer Big Macs, but I would never bring one and hurt Mrs. Gretzky's feelings. Big Macs are Lech's favorite food.

"Oof," Mrs. Gretzky said, sitting down heavily in her chair at the head of the table. She sighed deeply and took a few deep breaths. I found a cushion and slid it under her feet. I know it helps if she keeps them up.

"Bless you," she said.

We all bowed our heads and Mrs. Gretzky said grace. Everyone took a bite and told Mrs. Gretzky how delicious her food was.

Then I said, "I agree with Porsha. Barbara was murdered and it seems like the police and some powerful people want to forget about it. Well, speaking just for myself, I'll never forget about it."

"You think Sink killed her?" Porsha asked, pulling a toothpick out of her cabbage roll. "To stop the sexual harassment suit? It wouldn't look good for a politician to have stuff like that going down. Accusations. Bad press. Women complaining."

"Maybe somewhere else it wouldn't," I said. "But in this neighborhood, in our ward, I don't think it would matter all that much. I know on TV you see big famous politicians in trouble over their sex lives. But here—in the neighborhood—well, being a dirty old man might lose him a few votes, but no way would Sink lose an election over it. And even if he did, would Sink murder someone to win an election? I don't think so." I remembered the pathetic-dog look on Sink's face when— for a moment—he thought he'd made me feel bad. Sink was a kindly man. He had faults, plenty of them. But I didn't see him as a murderer.

"Alderman Synko will be big man around here until the day he dies," Mrs. Gretzky agreed. "He won't lose the election for doing the same as most of the men in the neighborhood would like to do if they got the chance. Sally, I forgot the salt and pepper."

Sally jumped up, scurried off to the kitchen, and returned a moment later with salt and pepper shakers. Mrs. Gretzky took the salt cellar and shook it hard over her mashed potatoes.

"Okay, then, I hope you won't mind me saying this," Porsha said, "but what about Janet's brother Dennis? Maybe he's the one Barbara was meeting in the forest preserve and they argued about the lawsuit and he walloped her." She turned to me. "Sorry, Janet. Just thinking out loud."

"That's okay," I said. "I'm not close to my brother, and I don't know him all that well. He's twelve years older and by the time I was old enough to really talk to him, he'd left home. But when I went to see him, he acted like he was real fond of Barbara. I could tell he was upset about her death. And I got the feeling that he was going to make good money off the suit against Sink. Now that she's dead, he won't be able to. So her dying—that's not good news for Dennis any way you look at it."

We all ate in silence for a moment. Lech came slinking in and slid under Sally's chair. He knows she is a soft touch and if anyone was going to give him table scraps, it would be Sally. But Lech knows Mrs. Gretzky doesn't approve. He can get table scraps in the kitchen, but not in her living room with her special carpet with the roses and crowns on it that she got from her mother. Mrs. Gretzky doesn't want grease on that. She gave Sally a warning look. Sally looked innocent, but I saw her hand snake down under the table and heard a slurping sound.

"Here's what I think," Porsha said. "We don't know anything about Barbara or about her life, and she could have lots of enemies. I say we investigate."

"Alderman Synko and Janet's brother Dennis, they don't want an investigation," Mrs. Gretzky said. "One thing I bet you, they both have secrets they want to hide. We get in their way, they could make life hard for us."

"How?" Porsha said.

"The W.R.C. is a business," Mrs. Gretzky said, "and a business needs permits. It pays taxes and gets services from the city. You don't want to cross the alderman from your ward if you can help it."

"I don't care," Porsha said. "We should show them they can't tell us what to do. *They* say accident. *We* say murder. Let's investigate. We'll prove we're right. We'll find out who did this and see that they pay."

Mrs. Gretzky said, "You need to think a little. Someone who, when he doesn't like what's going on, smashes people on the head. That someone is out there. You cross him. Then what?"

We were all quiet for a moment. In the silence I heard the low rumble of thunder.

Then I said, "We have to do it. We have to investigate. Sink and Dennis, they're hiding something."

"Can you get Larry to help us?" Sally asked me.

"Larry has someone new," I said.

"Oh, Janet!" Sally said. "Are you sure?"

Everyone looked at me. "I saw them together," I said. "She's blond and beautiful and looks like a women's basketball star or something."

"She messes with Larry, I'll slam-dunk her myself," Porsha said.

"I don't get it. Larry is crazy about you," Sally said. "Did he say it to your face? Did he tell you it's over? You can get him back. Maybe just pretend like you don't know about her and he'll come back to you."

"Too late for that plan," I said. "He said he'll call, but I know he won't."

I looked at my backpack. My cellular phone was in it. The only people who had my cell number were my W.R.C. friends and Larry.

Ring, I thought to myself, looking at the backpack, wishing hard as I had off and on all day.

The phone rang.

I stared at my backpack. My mouth dropped open.

"Oh my God!" screamed Sally. "Your cell phone's ringing. It's Larry. Right now. Can you believe it!"

"It can't be," I mumbled. I reached into the backpack, grabbed the phone, and flicked it open. "Hello?" I said, my voice cracking.

"Janet?" Larry's voice said. "I've got to talk to you."

CHAPTER 5

Once we decided to investigate Barbara's death, we didn't waste any time.

The day after our dinner, the W.R.C. sprang into action. Officially there were only four of us. But when my friends and I got going, we could spread through the neighborhood the way mint takes over a garden.

This was the plan. Porsha would get her teenage friends to snoop around. They would ask questions about Barbara—like who she hung out with, or if she'd been seen with any known criminals lately. Mrs. Gretzky had her old friends from her church. She'd see what they knew. The beauty shop where Sally worked, Hair-Today, was the neighborhood gossip central, so Sally would ask her most chatty clients about Barbara Noyes. Then she could just sit back and listen as the ladies talked up a storm.

Of course, we knew that some of what we heard

would be wrong, but it was a start.

We had decided that our best source would be Tiffany. So I called her and asked her to have lunch with me.

"Sorry. Can't. I can't leave the office," Tiffany told me. "This place is a zoo without Barbara."

"You have to eat," I said. "Might as well have lunch with me."

"Take-out at my desk," Tiffany said. "That's it. I'm working ten-hour days. We've got to reassure people. There's lots of rumors going around." She lowered her voice to a whisper. "The guys here are blaming you, Janet, you and the W.R.C. Why are you telling everybody Barbara was murdered? It makes the alderman look bad."

"What? Tiffany! I don't believe you. I thought you wanted us to find out who did it. *You* more than anybody. *You* believe it was murder. You told me so."

"Don't say that," Tiffany hissed. "You'll get me in big trouble."

"I don't understand you," I said. "Why have you changed your mind?"

"Okay, okay, we better meet. How about after I get off work? Say six o'clock."

"I can't," I said. I was having dinner with Larry. He had invited me and I had accepted. I should have felt good about it, but I didn't. Larry had sounded strange on the phone. He had said he had something to tell me and I didn't like the sound of that. He was going to break up with me for the blond with the braid. I just knew it.

"Oh, all right!" Tiffany said. "Lunch. I'll meet you at Pizza Pizza at noon. The one behind our office."

I hung up the phone at my desk at the W.R.C. Since it was Thursday, Sally was in the office. She worked at

Hair-Today noon to eight on Thursdays, so she could come into the W.R.C. in the morning. "Tiffany doesn't want to talk to me. She acted weird," I said to Sally.

"I don't get it," Sally replied. "Tiffany was so hot to find out who murdered Barbara, you'd think she'd want to help any way she could."

"I know," I said. "Probably Sink got on her case. I don't see Tiffany standing up to Sink if he puts pressure on her."

"She's not strong like you are, Janet," Sally said.

Sally has this crazy idea that I am a tough woman. All my life I've longed to be considered tough, and now that it's happened, I find out that it feels like there's two of me. There's the Janet Barkin people come to and ask for help—the Janet Barkin that Sally thinks she knows—and then there's the real Janet Barkin—the scared, doubting, fat one who didn't finish high school.

"Sure, strong," I said. "That's why I almost fell apart when Larry called. I hear his voice and I turn into jelly."

"That's not about strong or weak," Sally said. "That's about love."

Lech, who was lying under my desk dozing, lifted his head and looked at the door. It opened and a teenage boy peered in. He stood there, holding the door open for a moment, looking around the office. Then he entered.

He was a tall, skinny kid, fourteen or fifteen, wearing baggy pants low on his hips and flashy new Nike sneakers. He wore his dishwasher-blond hair in a short buzz cut, and he had a little gold ring in his eyebrow. His nose looked funny somehow.

He looked back and forth between Sally and me. He shifted his weight from one foot to another.

Lech looked up at him for a moment, then let out a sigh and dropped his head back onto his paws.

"May I help you?" I asked.

"Uh, yeah. Maybe. I don't know. Oh, forget about it. This is a bad idea," the kid said. He turned toward the door and opened it. Then he shut it, came back, and sat on the chair next to my desk.

"You're Janet Barkin, right?" he said.

"Yes."

"You're, like, the boss of the W.R.C.?"

"Yes. Is there a problem we can help you with?"

He darted his eyes toward Sally. "Who's she?" he said. He tried to make his voice tough, but it broke and came out partly deep and partly in a squeak. He blushed.

"That's Sally Lee. She works here too. She's one of the founders of the W.R.C."

The kid looked at Sally again and she smiled at him. Sally is very beautiful and the kid blushed again.

"Whatever," he said.

I waited.

He moved restlessly. Then he said, "It's about my sister. Would it, like, cost a lot of money for you to, like, see that my sister doesn't get fired?"

"Why don't you tell me what the problem is?" I said.

"My sister . . ."

"First, maybe you could tell me your name and her name?" I said.

"Oh! Sorry. I'm Tod Spears. My sister is Cheryl Spears. She works at Bauer Construction."

"I know them," I said. "They do a lot of the construction work around here. I think they own quite a bit of real estate in the neighborhood too."

"Mr. Bauer is into a lot of stuff. He owns, like, strip

malls. Like this one? And gets a lot of contracts. And runs big projects? He's, like, really tight with Alderman Synko?"

"I know who Alderman Synko is," I said.

"Cheryl, my sister? She works in the office at Bauer Construction. She takes the calls and keeps track of the work crews and she's, like, Mr. Bauer calls her his 'girl Friday'?"

"That sounds like a good job," I said.

"It is!" Tod said. "And here's the thing. My sister and me, well, our parents are, like, troubled, you know? My dad drinks and beats on my mom and stuff like that, and Human Services took Cheryl and me away from them. Right?"

I nodded.

"And we had to stay in foster homes. Different ones. Cheryl's a lot older than me. And she got into trouble and got picked up by the cops tons of times, know what I mean?"

"I understand," I said.

"And then Cheryl decided to turn it around." He blushed. "Because of me. Because I was staying with these like, really gross people, and the guy he, like, beat me and stuff. And Cheryl decided to get it together and make a home for her and me, okay?"

"That sounds wonderful," I said.

"Yeah. Wonderful. But no one would give her a job, so this, like, really uptight Human Services lady wouldn't let Cheryl and me live together in our own apartment. Because, like, even though she was over twenty-one, how could she support us?"

I nodded.

"But then Alderman Synko found Cheryl this job

with Mr. Bauer. And she made good money and got an apartment and Miss Mumford let me live with Cheryl and everything was cool."

Tod turned away from me to take a quick, admiring look at Sally, and I saw what had been bothering me about his nose. It had been broken and healed up crooked. I wondered if it was his father or his foster father who had broken it, and I felt sad.

"Cheryl is very responsible," Tod assured me. "She follows all the rules Miss Mumford gave us. She cooks real good and keeps the place clean and stuff. And last term I got a perfect attendance record at school. I'm going to be a mechanic." He looked down at his hands. "I like to fix cars, you know?"

"Sounds like you two have really turned your lives around," I said.

"We're working on it," Tod said. "But now, something's wrong. Cheryl—she's losing it. When she comes home from work, every night now, she's, like, real angry. Last night she was drinking and she's not supposed to. She hasn't for a long time and if Miss Mumford finds out, or if she loses her job, they'll make me go back to the foster home." He balled his fists. "I won't let them do that. I'd just go back on the street. I know how to make it there. Good luck finding me. But I can't go back to the street, because I have to take care of Cheryl. I have to be there for her, like she was for me."

"What's wrong with Cheryl?"

Tod looked me right in the eye for the first time. He had a child's eyes. They were wide and blue and clear and they pierced my heart. I've had my troubles with my family. My mama died when I was a little girl and I didn't get along with my dad or my brother. But I never had to put up with anything like Tod and Cheryl had experienced.

"I don't know!" Tod said. "Something bad is going on at work. The other day, I saw a cop talking to Cheryl. They were, like, arguing. Outside our building. When I asked her about it, she wouldn't tell me anything. I think she's in trouble."

"Why are you scared she'll be fired from Bauer's?"

"All of a sudden she's real cheap. We used to have good food for supper. Like burgers and fried chicken and even spaghetti and meat sauce. But now she just buys lunch meat and macaroni and cheese in boxes. So I go, 'Why do we have to eat this slop?' And she says she has to save for a rainy day. And I'm like, 'Rainy day? What rainy day?' And she's like, 'When I lose my job, dopey, that rainy day!' And I'm like, 'Who says you're going to lose your job?' And she's like, 'Shut up, dopey!'"

"What do you want the W.R.C. to do?" I asked.

"Find out what's wrong. You protect women, right? Everyone says you're the ones who help women in trouble. Cheryl's in trouble. If she loses the job at Bauer's, who's gonna hire her? With her record? And being fired from Bauer's? I don't see Sink, like, finding her another job if he thinks she blew this one. No, something bad is going down at Bauer's and Cheryl's getting screwed. I know it. My sister would do anything to keep her job. She's scared. You've got to do something before they can her."

"Okay, okay, calm down," I said.

"You'll help?"

"I can't promise, Tod. But we'll check it out. We'll do our best."

His tight, scared face broke into a big smile. "Cool."

"Can I have your number?" I asked. "I'll phone when I know something."

"Hey, no way. I don't want Cheryl to know I came here. She'd kill me. I'll come by tomorrow on my way home from school."

"That will work," I said.

"But wait. How much will it cost?"

"Don't worry about it," I said. "Mrs. Christian, the lady who founded W.R.C., lets us take on worthy cases when people can't pay." This was a lie, as there was no Mrs. Christian. We had made her up to explain where our money came from because we didn't want people to know about the lottery money behind the W.R.C.

"Then I'm outta here," Tod said. He reached down and patted Lech. "Neat dog." Then he turned and sauntered out the door. His step was much lighter than it had been when he came in.

I, on the other hand, was not that cheery. "Sally, what do you think?"

"Cute kid," Sally said. "His story was so sad. I'm glad we're going to try to help."

"Yes . . ." I said.

"What's the matter?" Sally asked.

"I don't know. I have a funny feeling about this. Bauer Construction. Alderman Synko. Notice how those names keep cropping up?"

"Of course they do," Sally said. "Alderman Synko practically runs the ward. And Bauer Construction is one of the biggest employers in the neighborhood."

"You're probably right," I said.

But I didn't think she was.

CHAPTER 6

Pizza Pizza smelled terrific. In my opinion, a person can never get enough pizza. My favorite is deep-dish pizza, loaded: Italian sausage, ham, pepperoni, veggies, pineapple, the works. I topped mine off with a heavy layer of grated Parmesan from the bottle on the table.

Tiffany, I noticed, was not enjoying her pizza. She was picking bits off it and eating them slowly. She'd eat a piece of sausage, then a chunk of green pepper, then a mushroom. Her pizza looked like the cat had been at it.

"It's not like it seems," Tiffany said.

For a moment I thought she meant her pizza. I swallowed and wiped my greasy hands on my napkin. Then I got it. "You mean you changing your mind about Barbara?" I asked.

"I didn't exactly change my mind," Tiffany said. She was wearing a black T-shirt with big red lips on it. Under the lips the writing said: "I'm lost! Please take me home."

"So do you still think she was murdered?" I demanded.

"Well, sure. No. I mean . . ."

"You saw her," I said. "I know I'll never forget how she looked."

Tiffany dropped the piece of ham she had in her hand. She swallowed, patted her lips with her napkin, and gagged slightly. "Don't talk it about! Don't remind me."

"You said you felt responsible," I continued. "I can't understand how you can be part of this cover-up Sink and Dennis are into."

"Cover-up?" Tiffany said weakly. She pulled a corner off her napkin and rolled into a little ball.

"Cover-up!" I said firmly. "That's what's going on. The question is, why?"

"I don't know anything about any cover-up," Tiffany mumbled. She tore another piece off her napkin and rolled it into an even smaller ball.

"What's the matter, Tiffany," I said softly. "What are you afraid of?"

Tiffany smiled weakly. She rolled the little napkin balls around the table with her finger. Some of her fingernails were bright red and some were black. They matched the colors on her T-shirt. "I guess," she said, "I'm afraid of everything. That's the trouble with me." Her eyes got teary. "I get scared easy. I've always been like this." She picked up her torn napkin and dabbed at her eyes, smearing her mascara. "I bet I look a mess," she sniffled.

"Is it Sink?" I asked.

"Yeah. Sink. Dennis. The new office manager, all of them. Everybody's on my case. They say it's my fault the W.R.C. is going around stirring things up. Asking questions. Making Sink look bad. All's we want is for this thing to die down."

"By 'this thing,' you mean Barbara's murder?" I asked.

"They say I'd better not rock the boat. I'm supposed to shut up and keep my head down. Sink says I owe it to him and to the ward. Loyalty is everything in politics, you know. There's friends and there's enemies. Sink told me I have to choose which side I'm on and decide if I'm his friend or his enemy."

"Which did you choose?"

"Friend! Of course, I picked friend. I love Sink. Everybody does."

"You sure about that? Did Barbara? I know she was suing him."

"Oh that," Tiffany said. "That was a big joke. Sink treated Barbara better than anyone. He's always got his hand on your butt or your leg or something. He doesn't mean anything by it. But he didn't do that to Barbara."

"So why was she suing him?"

"I told you I didn't like her! I told you she was a bitch! Oh God, I shouldn't say that, she's dead." Tears ran down Tiffany's face. "It's all such a mess."

"You've got something on your mind. Tell me."

"Sink told me to box up all her files and give them to him," Tiffany said. She picked up her purse and took out a little package of tissues. She removed one and wiped carefully under her eyes, removing the smeared mascara. "Then a registered letter came from Dennis telling us not to touch Barbara's files. He was coming to get them. Sink told me to ignore Dennis's letter. He said Barbara worked for him and the files were his. He said Dennis was out of line."

"Maybe that's right," I said thoughtfully.

"Barbara had files that related to ward business. I can see Sink had a right to those. But also, she had other files of her own—which were the ones Dennis wanted. And those are exactly the ones Sink didn't want Dennis to have. He asked me to bring them into his office." Tiffany swallowed hard, as if she had bitten off too big a piece of pizza. "I did it," she said. "That same night, Sink came in after dinner and went through her files. He put some back in Barbara's file drawer and took some. So when Dennis showed up, he took the ones in the drawer. He thinks he's got all of them. He doesn't. Janet, could I get in trouble?"

"Maybe," I said. "Do you know what was in the files Sink kept?"

"Are you kidding? Barbara kept her files locked. She treated them like they were the secrets of the universe or something. Nobody looked at her files or touched them."

"How did you get them to give to Sink?"

"I guess the keys to her file drawers were on her body," Tiffany said. "Sink got them back from the police and he gave them to me."

"Where are the files now?" I asked. "The ones Sink kept."

"In his office," Tiffany replied.

"Does he keep his office locked?"

"Yes, but I have a key."

"I need to see those files," I said.

"Oh, no way. Oh, no. Don't ask me. Please."

"I'm asking you," I said looking right at her. "We need to know what's going on. We need to know what Sink is hiding, what Barbara was up to, and who her enemies were."

"Why?" Tiffany cried. Her voice was so loud that, even in the clamor of Pizza Pizza, the people at nearby tables turned to stare.

"Why do we need to know?" Tiffany repeated in a softer voice.

I didn't say anything. I just looked at Tiffany. I let her conscience answer the question.

"Oh all right, all right, all right! But if we're going to do it, let's get it over with quick, okay? Or else I'll have a heart attack. I can't take this. Tonight, after everybody's gone."

"It'll have to be late," I said, thinking of my "date" with Larry.

"How about midnight?" Tiffany said. "Sink's staff works late but for sure everyone will be gone by then."

"Fine," I said.

"I'm not walking around alone on the streets that late," Tiffany said. "You have to come pick me up at my apartment."

I could borrow a car. "I'll be at your place at a quarter to twelve," I said.

Tiffany was sniffling again. "Do we really have to do this?" she asked me.

"Yes," I said, "we do."

*   *   *

Larry and I drove along Sheridan Road into the city. It was dark and lights sparkled from boats in the lake. A fine rain was falling, and Larry couldn't get the windshield wipers to go at the right speed. Sometimes they went fast and then they squeaked. Or they went too slow and water beaded up so you could hardly see out the window.

"I thought we might have a tornado today," Larry said. "All day long it felt so still and heavy. Like the barometer dropped."

"Don't we mostly get tornadoes in the summer?" I asked. Larry looked very handsome. He was wearing a light blue shirt, ironed khaki pants, and a soft suede jacket. It was hard for me to see him sitting there so close and know that I shouldn't reach out to touch him. He was being too polite, talking about the weather. My heart was beating and my hands were sweaty. When was he going to break the bad news? Why didn't he just say he wanted to dump me and get it over with?

"Oh, who cares about tornadoes!" Larry said suddenly, slamming his hand on the steering wheel. The car swerved. "Shit. I'm sorry, Janet. Listen, about the way I've been acting . . ." He glanced at me. I didn't say anything. "I wish I could explain, but I just can't, that's all," he said.

"If you want to tell me it's over between us, why don't you just do it," I said.

"Over?" Larry shouted. "What are you saying?" He took a deep breath. "Nothing has changed—at least not on my side."

"Does that mean you've been flirting with blond sexpots all this time?" I said. I don't know why I said that. It just popped out.

I looked at Larry's face and I could see he was mad. His mouth was in a tight, hard line. "I was not flirting with a blond sexpot!" he said, his teeth clenched. "Cheryl is just a friend."

"Cheryl?" I said.

"Cheryl Spears. An old friend," Larry said.

I knew he was lying. He knew I knew he was lying.

"Fine. Okay. Do whatever you want," I said. I looked out the window. It was raining harder now.

"Listen, Janet, can we talk about something else for a moment?"

"Whatever," I said.

"You know the Barbara Noyes investigation?"

"Of course I do. I found the body and I was at the station answering questions and signing stuff for hours."

"I hear you're going around saying it wasn't an accident."

"The W.R.C. doesn't believe that accident story," I said. "We're investigating like we did on those other two cases, the ones you helped us with. The ones you made the arrests on." I didn't add, *and the ones that helped you get promoted to detective.*

"What have you found out?" Larry asked.

"Nothing yet."

Larry looked at me. I could tell he was trying to figure out if I was speaking the truth or not. Then he said, "You didn't ask for my help this time."

"You didn't return my calls this time," I said.

"What a mess," Larry said. "I want to explain it all to you. I want you to trust me, but it's better for both of us if you're mad at me." A little smile appeared for a moment on his face, then disappeared to be replaced by a look of sadness.

"You want me to trust you so you can find out what I know about Barbara Noyes, is that what this is about?" I asked.

We were passing Lincoln Park. Larry suddenly swerved into the park and stopped the car, and with the engine turned off, I could hear the rain clattering on the roof. It ran down the windows so I couldn't look out.

"That's not fair, Janet," Larry said. "You know I care for you."

"I thought you did," I said.

Larry reached out for me, pulled me to him. His arms went around me and the familiar wonderful feeling filled my body. I hugged him back and it felt so good. Everything had to be all right. There would be an explanation for Larry's weird behavior. I only needed to trust him and he would explain everything when he could.

Larry pulled back and looked at me. "I shouldn't be doing this. I shouldn't be taking you out. We can't see each other right now."

"Okay," I said, snuggling back into his arms. "But when can we see each other again?"

He squeezed me tightly to him, then he released me and sat up. I felt him withdrawing so I sat back on my side of the car. He started up the engine and pulled back onto the road.

"When?" I repeated.

"I don't know," Larry said. "Soon, I hope." But he didn't look at me; he kept his eyes on the road.

The good feeling drained out of me. I stared at his profile. His lips were set tight, his eyes staring straight ahead, and I knew he was hiding something.

The blond with the braid was Cheryl Spears, Tod's sister. She worked at Bauer Construction. Bauer Construction—the place Alderman Synko kept finding jobs for people.

Tod had said his sister was arguing with a cop. Larry was a cop. It all fit together somehow.

But how?

And however it fit together, why would any of it keep

Larry from dating me? His excuse sounded fishy and it felt fishy. I had trusted my ex-husband, Pat, and he had lied to me and cheated on me. Obviously, all a man had to do was spin me a line and I fell for it.

Well, not anymore. Once fooled, twice shy. Only a fool makes the same mistake twice.

"It's not good enough, Larry," I said.

The rain fell harder and the windshield was so filled with water I couldn't see out. It made me feel blind.

And I had no idea what Larry was up to. But I intended to find out.

*   *   *

Two hours later I was back in my apartment. Larry and I had had dinner and tried to act like friends, but it hadn't been easy and it hadn't been fun.

I didn't have much time before I had to meet Tiffany. Changing into jeans and a black sweatshirt, grabbing a poop-scoop and a plastic bag, I called to Lech.

"Come on, Lech. Let's take you for a walk before we go break into Alderman Synko's office," I said to him.

He looked up at me.

"I know, I know," I said. "You can tell I'm feeling blue. It's because of Larry, but I've got to be tough. I can't go running after a man who doesn't want me." I was standing at the front door, my hand on the knob.

Lech pushed his nose into my knee. It was a gentle push—kind of a doggy version of a comforting hug.

"I know you love me, Lech," I said. "I appreciate it. But I'm going to miss Larry."

Lech sat down and cocked his head to one side. His eyes said, *tell me about it*.

"Larry didn't say it's over between us, but you have to

face facts," I explained. "The way he acted, what else could it mean? It's probably all for the best. I wouldn't want to spy on a man I was going with. But look at it this way, Lech. Larry is involved with Cheryl and Cheryl works at Bauer's. Bauer's company is connected somehow to Alderman Synko and Barbara worked for Alderman Synko. One thing links to another, see what I mean?"

I could tell Lech agreed with me. It all looked very suspicious. We had to find out what was going on and that might mean spying on Larry.

Lech might not want to believe me now, but sooner or later he would have to accept the obvious fact. The romance between Larry and me was finished.

CHAPTER 7

I parked the car and Tiffany and I got out. The sound of the doors slamming was very loud on the quiet street. As we headed down the street to the ward office, I could hear our footsteps echoing on the sidewalk. Tiffany's high-heeled boots clunked heavily while the pattering of Lech's paws sounded surprisingly loud and even my sneakers seemed to make a thudding noise.

Most of the storefronts were lit up, but a few—storefront medical clinics, accounting and law offices—were dark. As we came closer to Sink's office, on the other side of the street, I saw it too was dark.

"Let's get this over with," Tiffany said, her voice high and nervous. She opened her purse and took out a key ring.

"No, wait," I said. "We need to check around first. Be sure there's nobody still working."

Tiffany approached the storefront and peered in through the plate-glass window. "It's dark. There's no one in there. I can tell."

"You can't see everything," I said. "There might be someone in the back, in Sink's office. And what about your photocopy-kitchen area? You can't see that from the front."

I remembered the layout of the ward offices. There was a large open front room with six desks in it plus visitor chairs, tables with literature on them, a water cooler, and a bookshelf. In the back of this large room was a door that opened onto a wide hall. On one side of the hall was a sink and countertop where they made their coffee. On the other side was a photocopier, a table for collating and folding, and several file cabinets. At the back of this hall, a door led to Sink's office, which had a casement window overlooking the alley behind. "I'll go around and check the back," I said.

"No, don't leave me here," Tiffany said nervously, looking up and down the street. "I don't like being out alone in this neighborhood."

"I'll tell Lech to stay with you," I said. I turned to him. "Lech, stay! Guard Tiffany!"

Lech moved into position next to Tiffany, his ears alert as I headed down the passageway between storefronts that led to the alley. "Don't take too long!" Tiffany called after me.

I turned my flashlight on, shining its beam before me. It produced a thin channel of light, so I seemed to be walking between walls of dark shadow. I heard a sudden rustle and I started as something scurried past me. A rat?

I came out onto the alley, turned right, and walked until I was near where I expected the alderman's office to be. I shone my light on a back door. Bull's-eye. A tattered poster of Alderman Synko was stuck to the door. I turned off my flashlight and walked toward the door. As I neared it, I thought I saw a glimmer of light shining out of Sink's back office window.

I wished I had Lech with me, because Lech always knew when there was hidden danger. I slowed my steps and edged closer to the buildings, so there was no chance I could be seen by someone looking out of Sink's back window.

My foot struck something and I stumbled. In the poorly lit alley, I could just make out a stack of cardboard boxes as they tipped over, falling against the building. Soft-drink cans tumbled out into the alley with a clatter and the glimmer of light disappeared from the back window of Sink's office. Had the noise scared someone off? Or had I imagined the light inside? It could have been a reflection of one of the security lights shining off buildings on the other side of the alley.

I sneaked along the alley wall to the window and peered into Sink's office. There were blinds on the window, but they were open. Through them, I could see the dark shapes of furniture.

I peered in, trying to decide if anyone was in there. I thought of Tiffany, waiting in front. She must be getting even more scared. She was an awfully fearful person considering those in-your-face T-shirts she wore. The one she had picked for our midnight break-in had a picture of a gingerbread man on it. Underneath him it said: "The perfect man. If he makes you mad, you can just bite his head off."

Nothing stirred in Sink's office. I turned on my flashlight, pointed it into the room, and moved it so I could see all around. I saw Sink's desk, chair, file cabinets. The desk sat in the middle of the room and the back of his chair faced me. I pointed the flashlight into the corners of the room—no one was there. In one corner there was a pile of document boxes, the kind that are designed to hold file folders.

Bingo.

I headed back down the alley, trying to avoid the spilled soda cans.

"What took you so long?" Tiffany called as I came out onto the street. She was shivering, her arms wrapped around her chest. "It's cold. Let's do it, okay? I want to get this over with."

She handed me her key ring and I opened the door to the office, standing back so Lech could go in first.

He bounded inside, then froze. "What's the matter, Lech?" I said. "Is anybody here?"

I stepped inside. Tiffany followed, closing the door behind her. I shone the flashlight quickly around the room. It was empty.

Lech looked at me, then streaked to the door at the back of the room and sniffed it, then made a growling noise. "What is it?" I asked him.

"Maybe you shouldn't open that door," Tiffany said in a quavery voice.

"Aren't the file cabinets back there? And Sink's office?" I asked.

"Yes, but . . . look at Lech."

I walked across the room to the door and, standing to the side, reached over and turned the knob and flung it open. Lech leapt inside. He scurried around the hallway, sniffing, then raced to the door at the back of the hall, the door that led to Alderman Synko's office. He stood by the door at attention and growled.

"Lech thinks there's somebody in Sink's office," I said. "But I just looked into it from the alley and it's empty."

"I want to go home, Janet," Tiffany whispered. "I really do."

"What's the matter, Lech?" I asked. "Someone you don't trust been here?" I turned to Tiffany. "If people are very angry or upset or hostile, they send out special smells that Lech recognizes. He knows those smells means danger and he can detect them even after the hostile person is gone." I turned to him. "Is that what's bothering you, Lech?" I asked.

Lech growled again, pointing his nose toward Sink's office door.

"Which is the key to Sink's office?" I asked Tiffany, holding up the key ring she had given me.

"That one," she said pointing. "You're not going in there, are you?"

"I told you," I said. "I looked and there is no one there."

"What was that?" Tiffany hissed.

"What?"

"I thought I heard a door shut."

I unlocked Sink's door. "Stand over there," I said to Tiffany. Worst case, if someone in Sink's office came flying out or let off a shot, I didn't want Tiffany in the line of fire. Of course, I was sure there was no one there, but why take chances? "Lech probably smells someone who is long gone," I said.

"Can Lech smell through doors?" Tiffany pressed herself against the same wall the back door was on, as far away from Sink's office door as she could get.

I didn't answer. I stood out of the line of sight from the door and swung it open.

Lech bounded into Sink's office. "Anybody there?" I asked Lech.

I heard him moving about. I waited a moment, then peered in, shining my flashlight around. Lech was standing in the middle of the room looking at the back door, and I could tell from the way he stood that he thought there was no danger in the room.

"See? I told you there was no one here," I said, realizing I had been holding my breath and letting it out noisily. "You can come in."

Tiffany entered. She waved at the document boxes in the corner. "That's where Sink put the files he didn't give to Dennis." She switched the light on.

"Turn that off!" I snapped. "We don't want anyone to know we're here."

"Sorry, sorry, sorry," Tiffany said, flicking the switch so that the room returned to darkness.

A faint glimmer of light came in from the alley. I went to the back window and looked out. Security lights mounted on a few buildings cast pools of light, but most of the alley was dark. I stared at one darkened area where I thought I saw something moving. I watched but nothing happened and no one stirred.

Tiffany opened the document boxes and flipped through the files inside. "What are we looking for?" she asked.

I came over and squatted down beside her. She was shining her flashlight on the files. "These are Barbara's files," Tiffany said. "I took them out of the drawers and put them into boxes. A box for each file drawer. But I didn't really look at them. I was scared to."

"Why?" I asked. "She couldn't care now."

"I know it was silly of me, but I'm superstitious and I don't like touching dead folks' things." Tiffany laughed nervously. "Barbara had her own system. She color-coded the tabs. No one else was allowed to touch her files."

Tiffany leafed through the files, reading the labels printed on the tabs. It seemed as if her superstition had faded away. "Wow! Look at this. She has a whole hanging-file section labeled 'Sexual Harassment.'"

I peered over her shoulder. "Those sure are neat files," I said. They were green hanging file folders labeled with colored plastic tabs. Each green hanging file folder held a bunch of cream-colored folders. All the cream-colored folders had computer-printed labels on them.

"Is this what you're looking for?" Tiffany asked. "See? A hanging file, *Harassment, Pattern of.* Oh my God, look at this. She has a file in it with my name on it! And look here, there are more. What a sneak! She kept files on every woman in the office."

I looked beyond Tiffany's fingers to the next file.

"She's got a whole section on Bauer Construction!" I said. "We need to take them all out and look at them."

Lech barked. It was a special bark I recognized.

I jumped up, turning off my flashlight. "Tiffany, get out of here. Now! Go into the front of the office. Quick!"

Lech was standing facing the back door. Even in the dim light I could see that the fur around his neck had risen so that he looked twice his normal size.

Tiffany didn't move. She stayed frozen to the spot.

"Get out!" I yelled. "Go! Now!" I gave her a push. She moved toward the inner door, just as the back door burst open. Lech leapt through it into the alley, barking frantically.

I turned to check on Tiffany. She ran to the coffee-photocopy area, slamming the door behind her—trapping me in Sink's office. I could hear Lech, his barks echoing loudly in the alley.

The window slid open and a dark shape came through it. In the dim light, I saw that it was a man in a ski mask holding something big in his hand, something like a baseball bat.

"Lech! He's in here!" I screamed.

The man raised the bat and swung it at me.

Lech hurtled through the window into the office and flung himself upon the man, snarling.

The man was thrown against the window, but he swung his bat, trying to slam it down on Lech's back. Lech twisted his body, but did not let go. He was trained not to. He would hang on until I told him to let go or the man beat him to death.

"Lech!" I commanded. "Let go! Back up and guard!"

Lech must have loosened his hold, because the man gave a sudden wriggle. With a smooth graceful movement, he twisted around, put his hands on the windowsill, pulled himself up, and vaulted over into the alley.

"Janet! Help!" Tiffany called.

Lech let loose with a sound that was half a growl and half a whimper. I could see he was hurt, but it must not have been too bad because he raced for the back door. Out he went, after the bad guy.

I opened the inner door. The light was on. Tiffany was huddled in the corner, shaking. "Thank God, thank God, you're okay," she sobbed as she saw me.

"What's the matter?" I snapped at her. "Is there someone in here?"

"No, no, I was just so scared, I heard you shouting and Lech barking . . ."

I took a quick look around. Tiffany was alone.

I ran back into Sink's office and then out the back door into the alley. "Lech!" I called.

He barked and I saw him, just a few yards away. He had jumped up so that his front legs were on the building. He was straining, clawing at the building as if—even hurt—he wanted to go up the wall. Had the bad guy climbed up onto the roof?

"Down!" I commanded. "Here!"

Immediately Lech dropped from the wall and trotted toward me. He dropped his head. He was ashamed and so was I—we had blown it and the bad guy had escaped. In the dark, I hadn't seen him well enough to recognize him if I saw him again. What a screw-up.

I knelt down and gently touched Lech's back. "That guy took quite a swing at you. Did he connect? Are you okay?" Lech looked up at me, then lowered his nose and licked my hand.

"You don't seem too badly hurt," I said, remembering how he had gone after the bad guy and jumped up on the wall. I ran my hands very gently over his back and he didn't flinch. "But take it easy until I get you to the vet and have you checked out."

I stood up. It felt creepy in the alley. As if someone was watching me. I shone my flashlight down the alley in one direction. I didn't see anyone. Then in the other. No sign of anyone that way either.

"Where did he go, Lech?" I asked my dog.

Lech ran to the place where he had been a moment before and looked up the wall.

"He climbed up there?" I said, shining my flashlight on the building. I saw a tall casement window with heavy, old-fashioned wooden trim. At second-story level, a fire escape ascended to the roof.

"I guess we lost him," I said. "That guy had strong arms and he could have swung up there from the window, I bet, and then gone up the fire escape. I guess that's a better way to lose a dog than running down an alley. I want to check the alley, though. Are you okay to walk?"

I beamed my light down the alley and Lech set off. I watched him. He didn't limp or seem seriously hurt. We walked down the alley to the end of the block, then back the other way. No one to be seen.

We re-entered the back office.

It was a shambles. Files lay spread around the file boxes. The boxes had been crushed. Papers were scattered everywhere. Furniture was smashed. Overturned. As if the intruder had been in a terrible rage and had swung his bat wildly in all directions. He must have come back while we were searching the alley!

"Tiffany!" I screamed.

We dashed into the middle hallway. Tiffany sat, huddled up in the corner where I had left her. Her head was buried in her hands. I could hear her gulping and sobbing, the way you do when you don't want anyone to hear you cry.

"Tiffany! Are you okay?"

"Is he gone?" she whispered.

"Who?" I asked.

Tiffany sobbed louder.

I opened the door to the front office and flashed my flashlight around. There was no one there.

"Whoever it was, he's gone," I said. "And there's no one in Sink's office now. What happened?"

She didn't raise her head from hands. "I don't know.

You and Lech went out the back and a minute later, a man came in the front. I guess I didn't lock it behind us. You shouldn't have left me alone. You said Lech would guard me."

"Someone came in the front door? Who?" I asked her.

"I didn't see him. I just heard him. I heard the door open. I thought at first it was you guys," Tiffany said, still not looking at me. "I'm sorry, Janet. I'm so sorry."

"Sorry for what?"

"For shutting the door on you. For freaking out. For not seeing who it was. But it was so horrible. I was sitting here. I heard the front door open. I was so happy because I thought it was you coming back and I yelled out, 'Janet?'

"Then this nasty voice goes, 'It's not Janet. Shut up. Press your face up against the wall and don't look, or I'll kill you.'

"I did it. I pressed my face against the wall and shut my eyes tight. I heard him walk by me and go into Sink's office. I didn't look. I heard terrible noises in there. Smashing. Crashing. I didn't move. I was, like, paralyzed."

"You didn't see him at all?"

"No."

"Recognize his voice?" I demanded, trying not to scold her. I could tell how terrified she was.

"No," she whimpered.

"Did he go back through the hall when he left? I didn't see him go out into the alley."

"Maybe he sneaked out when you weren't looking."

"Lech would have known."

"Maybe he came back through here while I had my eyes covered up," Tiffany said.

Weird. Her story was weird. "Tiffany, do you think you can come look at the files? See if you think anything's missing?"

"He's gone? You're sure he's gone? Don't you think we should phone 911?"

"No. I don't think we should phone 911," I said.

Calling to Lech, I went back into Sink's office. We shut and locked the back door. We shut and locked the back window. Then we went through the hall—where Tiffany still sat huddled in the corner, shaking—to the front office. We locked the front door, which was indeed unlocked. We checked the front window. It was solid plate glass and didn't open.

Returning to the Sink's office, I knelt down and looked through the files scattered over the floor. It only took me a few minutes to realize what had happened.

Barbara's sexual harassment files were gone.

CHAPTER 8

I was late for the meeting we had scheduled the next morning. It was a quarter after eight when I opened the front door to the W.R.C. office. Sally and Porsha were both waiting for me. Sally didn't start work at Hair-Today until ten, but Porsha had to leave for school at eight-thirty—which is why we were meeting so early.

Mrs. Gretzky's legs were giving her trouble. Since walking to the office was hard on her, we planned to fill her in by telephone.

"You look like something the cat dragged in," Porsha said.

"I feel worse," I replied, collapsing on my chair.

"I got us some doughnuts," Porsha said, putting a couple of chocolate doughnuts and a coffee on my desk. The doughnuts were my favorite kind, the ones with chocolate frosting and chocolate sprinkles. I looked down at them and didn't even feel like taking a bite.

Sally and Porsha were watching me. "That bad?" Porsha said. I usually grab at the first doughnut of the morning and scarf it down.

I sighed. "Worse. We blew it last night. Totally."

"What happened? Are you okay? Is Tiffany okay?" Sally asked.

"Our bodies are okay. Lech got beat up, but I took him to the vet this morning. He says it's nothing serious."

Lech had come in with me. Now he was lying curled up under my desk. Hearing his name, he thumped his tail on the floor. I reached down and petted him. Then I broke a piece off my doughnut and gave it to him. He ate it without enthusiasm. Lech doesn't really care for chocolate doughnuts. I think he eats them when I give him a piece because he doesn't want to hurt my feelings.

"Who beat up on you?" Porsha asked.

"To tell you the truth, I'm not really sure," I said. "Right from the moment I picked Tiffany up, she was nervous. Scared."

"That's your Tiffany," Porsha said. "No surprise there."

"First we checked out the ward office from the street," I continued. "Then I went around to the alley and looked in the back window, just to be sure no one was still working, you know? For a moment, I thought I saw someone in Sink's back office, but I decided I was wrong. That was my first mistake.

"Okay, so I decide the office is empty," I continued. "We go in through the front door. All clear. We head straight to the back office—which is Sink's—and start going through Barbara's files.

"All of a sudden, Lech goes bananas. The back door opens. Lech whips outside, leaving us alone in the back office. Then—it was *sooo* spooky—I see the window open and this dark shape slides into the room, like a monster in a horror movie."

Sally gasped. "Janet! You must have been scared out of your skull!"

"I shout for Lech and he comes running back in. He growls and jumps on the guy. The guy whaps Lech, slides out the window, and disappears."

"Unbelievable!" Sally said.

"Of course, Lech went after him. But it looked like the guy climbed a fire escape, went over the roof, and came down on the street side. Tiffany left the front door to the ward office open, so while I'm looking for him in the back alley, he comes in through the front door."

"Oh, no!" Sally said.

"Oh, yes. He scared Tiffany so bad she just curled up in the corner and shut her eyes. He said he would kill her if she peeked."

"I bet Tiffany caved," Porsha said.

"You can't blame her," I said. "Tiffany sat there in the hall, her eyes shut tight, not looking. The bad guy smashed up Sink's office and stole the files I was looking for. Also he swung at Lech and tried to hit him on the back, which I don't appreciate."

"Poor Lech!" Sally cried. She rushed over to him and hugged him.

Lech licked Sally's face and she returned the kiss. "Is he okay? What did the vet say?"

"He thinks he may be bruised, but it isn't serious. The bat just grazed him. And that's not all."

"There's more?" Sally asked.

"Yes. Last night, Larry and I broke up."

"No way!" Sally said. Now it was my turn to be

hugged. "You'll make up, I'm sure. He loves you."

"You'd never guess it by the way he acts," I said. "But one good thing. Tiffany and I had a chance to look through Barbara's files before the horror movie started. So I know which ones got taken."

I explained to Sally and Porsha about Barbara's filing system and how she had files on sexual harassment. I told them she had files on the sexual harassment of all the women in Sink's office, including Tiffany. Those were the very files that had been stolen.

"Hard to figure," Porsha said. "No point in Alderman Synko stealing files he already had. So it couldn't have been him."

"And I can't see Dennis doing it," I said. "He must already know what was in those files. Probably has copies of them. After all, he's Barbara's lawyer. I wonder if I should warn him. If he does have copies, he could be in danger too."

"Dennis can take care of himself," Sally said. Sally only knew Dennis a little, but what she knew she didn't like. She especially didn't like how he treated me in such a mean way. "The man who smashed up Alderman Synko's office and stole the files, you didn't get a look at him? No idea who he is?"

I shook my head, feeling frustrated. "It was dark. I saw this shape come through the window. I saw him swing something, maybe like a baseball bat." As I said this, I had an uneasy feeling as if I were missing something. I tried to get hold of the idea, but it slithered away. I continued. "Tiffany swears she never even peeked at him. There is something weird about her story, but she was a basket case last night, so I didn't push it. I need to talk to her again when she recovers. Can you believe it, she thought we should call 911?"

"That girl is a birdbrain," Porsha said. "I know you like her, Janet, but she is such a wimp. Call the cops and try to explain what you were doing in Sink's office at midnight? They'd probably blame you for trashing the place and stealing the files."

"I know," I said. "If we'd reported it, Sink would find out that we were there and we'd have to explain to him too."

"It'll be interesting to see if he tells anyone about the stolen files," Porsha said. She got up from where she had been sitting and swung her school bag onto her back. "Gotta go. I'll come by after school. Take care, and don't believe everything that Tiffany girl says. My take is, she's lying about a lot of things. Soft, wimpy people lie a lot. They don't have the guts to tell the truth and take their licks." She headed for the door. "By the way, kids should be coming by with reports today. The word is all around the neighborhood that the W.R.C. wants to know about Barbara and what's going down with Cheryl at Bauer's."

The door shut behind her. Sally and I looked at each other. "What do you think?" I asked Sally. "Do you trust Tiffany?"

"I know you like her," Sally said, "but I kind of agree with Porsha. Tiffany wears those in-your-face T-shirts, but somehow she seems like a person just waiting to be pushed around."

"I wasn't very nice to her last night," I admitted. "She fell apart when I needed her."

The front door opened. A woman entered. She wore a light brown suit with a red shirt and carried a big briefcase with the city crest on it. She was about forty-five, African-American, with perfectly styled hair, gold-rimmed glasses, and a stuck-up expression.

"Are you Janet Barkin?" she demanded.

"Yes," I said. "How may I help you?"

"I am Honoria Mumford," she said. She opened her purse, producing a little gold case. She snapped it open, took out a business card, and handed it to me. I thought that I would like to have a gold card case like that. I looked at the card. It had her name, the city crest, and a bunch of names and initials and titles on it. Enough to practically fill up the card.

"What can I do for you, Ms. Mumford?" I asked.

She sat down at the visitor chair next to my desk. "I'm with the Evanston Health and Human Services Department," she said. "I understand Tod Spears has been to see you and your office has been making inquiries about Bauer Construction and Cheryl Spears."

I glanced quickly at Sally.

"May I ask why you want to know?" I said.

"This so-called W.R.C.," Ms. Mumford said, looking around with disdain, "you're not connected with the city, is that right?"

"Yes, that's right," I replied.

"And no one here is a trained professional?"

"I'm not sure what you mean."

"Well, to be frank, I don't understand what you girls think you are doing," she said. "People without proper credentials shouldn't attempt to work with our more troubled and disadvantaged. You will do more harm than good."

"Proper credentials?" I said.

"I have a degree in social work *and* in behavioral psychology," she told me firmly.

I felt like saying, *and* I *have a drop-out degree from high school,* but I didn't. In fact, the way she looked at me and the W.R.C. office, it made me feel like I should report immediately to the principal. If this woman was Tod's case officer, he had real problems.

"What is your point, Ms. Mumford?" I said.

"It's my responsibility to be sure that Tod Spears does not come under harmful influence."

"By harmful influence, do you mean Tod's sister, Cheryl? It sounds to me like he loves her and she loves him and like she's working her tail off to make a home for him."

Mumford shifted uncomfortably in her chair when I said "working her tail off." I wondered if she would have given me a detention if I said "busting her butt" instead.

"Cheryl Spears has a history of serious problems," Mumford said, glaring at me.

"Like what?"

"Such as being found intoxicated and abusive in a public place. Such as being arrested for shoplifting, petty theft, and similar offenses."

"That was then," I said. "This is now. Cheryl has turned it around."

"I don't know where you are getting your information," Ms. Mumford said. "Cheryl Spears is a troublemaker at work and has caused our office a great deal of embarrassment. We work closely with Alderman Synko to place our clients in good jobs. We found a job for her at Bauer Construction. I'm sure you've heard of them as they are one of our most progressive and public-spirited employers. If she causes trouble at Bauer's, it makes it that much harder for us to place other clients there. You people asking questions of Bauer's employees about Barbara Noyes and Cheryl Spears is counterproductive."

Counterproductive? What did she mean? Did she

mean we were screwing up things for her?

"I'm very sorry to hear that," I said.

"The point I am trying to make is, you have no business involving yourself with Barbara Noyes' tragic death, nor with Cheryl Spears' affairs. And we would like you to cease. Immediately."

"I don't see why we should," I said.

"You surprise me, Ms. Barkin," Mumford said. I could see that she was holding on to her temper with difficulty. Her nasty little eyes glared at me from behind her gold-rimmed glasses. "I had assumed you had the best interests of these disadvantaged people at heart."

"How are we hurting their best interests?" I asked.

"Keep on the way you are, and you are sure to get Cheryl Spears fired," she spat out. "That's how!"

"And why are you bringing up Barbara Noyes?" I said. I thought if I pushed her a little harder, she might lose it and reveal what was really on her mind.

"Barbara Noyes' death is none of your business! Why can't you see that?"

"My brother, Dennis, said exactly the same thing. If he didn't stop us from finding out who murdered her, I don't see you stopping us either," I replied.

"Dennis? Dennis O'Hara? He's your brother?"

"Yes. Barkin is my married name. I used to be Janet O'Hara."

"My goodness. Dennis O'Hara is a great man," Mumford said, surprising me totally. Her face changed. The anger disappeared. "I had no idea," she added.

"Dennis? A great man?" I said.

"Singlehandedly, your brother has changed the climate for working women in this community. He has opened his door to women who are being sexually harassed. He has taken on their cases without any assurance he would make a penny. He has gone after their harassers and gotten big settlements when other lawyers wouldn't even look at their cases. Why, he has made some of our largest and most arrogant employers change their ways. And as part of the settlements, he has made sure that the firms open their doors to the possibility of hiring my clients. You should be proud of him, Ms. Barkin. I am sure you are." She smiled at me.

"Uh, yes," I said. I couldn't get over the way she had changed her tune.

She stood up. "I am sure you understand, Ms. Barkin. I only want the best for my clients. I want them to find good jobs and succeed. Keep your eye on the larger picture. Talk to your brother. He'll tell you I am right. Well, I think we understand each other." She picked up her briefcase, settled her purse strap on her shoulder, and left the office.

"Understand each other!" I said to Sally as soon as she was gone. "I have no idea what that witch was talking about! Do you?"

But before Sally could reply, all hell broke lose.

CHAPTER
9

The W.R.C. has three telephone lines and they all lit up. Sally and I each answered one while the other flashed threateningly.

The door burst open and several people came in. No sooner had we gotten rid of them when more arrived. For the rest of the day the office was like a bus station. The mailman came by with registered letters, inspectors from the city and from the state swarmed through the office like flies, and there was even someone from the feds. I think he was immigration—or tax. Whatever. FedEx and UPS both brought letters.

We were in trouble. Serious trouble.

It seemed that every department in the city and state was on our case. We were being inspected, requested to answer, scolded, studied, challenged, and insulted by more officials than I had ever known existed. We heard from youth officers, sanitary inspectors, health officials, animal welfare people, tax officials, environmental agents, water, sewer, electricity, gas, plumbing, fire, neighborhood planning, zoning—you name it. If the government had someone working on it, that person was asking us to explain how we were complying, telling us we were in breach, and issuing us warnings.

Mrs. Gretzky was getting it too. She called up from her apartment to say that she wasn't answering her phone anymore because she'd had more than she could take. The city licensing people and the tax people were threatening her. One good thing: Mrs. Gretzky wasn't upset, she was mad. The word she used was *persecution*. The other words she used were *Alderman Synko*.

"This is Alderman Synko's doing," Mrs. Gretzky shouted. I held the phone away from my ear. She was really mad. "Mark my words and write in a book!" Mrs. Gretzky yelled. "He's set all these busybodies after us! It's persecution, that's what it is!"

I thought she was right. I needed to talk to Sink and find out what the heck was going on.

The first time I managed to come up for air was late that afternoon. I guess inspectors and busybodies clock off at four-thirty. When the last of them had left and the office phones had stopped ringing, I picked up my cell phone and called Alderman Synko.

Tiffany answered the phone. "Tiff," I said, "it's Janet. I need to talk to Sink."

"Alderman Synko is not here at the present time," Tiffany said. She used a cold, official voice.

"Well, do you know when he will be there? Or is there a number I could get him at?" I asked.

"I am unable to give you that information," Tiffany said.

"Tiffany! What's the matter with you? Why are you

talking like that? I have to get in touch with Sink. Things are happening here and he must be behind them. You've got to help me. You owe it to me. You owe it to Barbara."

"Don't," Tiffany said. She sounded like she was about to cry. "Don't make me. I'm in enough trouble as it is."

"Tell me, Tiffany!" I said. I used the same voice I use when I give an order to Lech. My command voice.

"Sink is in a meeting with Mr. Bauer," Tiffany whispered. "But don't tell them I told you. And Janet?"

"What?"

Tiffany didn't answer. I could hear her breathing quickly into the phone—making little gaspy breaths. It sounded like she was crying.

"What's the matter, Tiffany?" I said gently. "If something's wrong, let me know. I'll try to help."

"Nobody can help me," Tiffany whimpered. "I screwed up. Bad."

"Come over to the W.R.C. office tonight after you get off work," I said.

"I can't. I'm too scared."

"The W.R.C. will help you," I said. "You'll see, everything will be okay."

"Okay, but don't tell anyone," Tiffany whispered, so softly I could barely hear her.

"You said Sink is with Mr. Bauer. How would I get in touch with him?" I knew I needed to talk to Bauer too. Might as well get it over with.

"I have Mr. Bauer's cell phone number," Tiffany whispered. "I'll give it to you. But you've got to promise . . ."

"Don't worry," I said. "Your secret is safe with me."

*   *   *

I picked my way over the muddy, churned-up earth at

the construction site. The site was surrounded with tall metal fencing. Construction had ended for the day and the partly-built office building was empty. In front of it was a temporary building, like a trailer. Steps led up to an open doorway. As I climbed, a light wind blew grit and dirt into my eyes.

I stepped into the darkened doorway and saw a man in a hard hat at a table writing.

"Mr. Bauer?" I said.

"What's it about?" the man at the table said.

"I'm Janet Barkin. We have an appointment."

"Matt!" yelled the man. "Lady here to see you. Says she has an appointment."

"Come in," a voice called.

The voice came from a doorway to my left. I went through the doorway and saw a man sitting at a desk. The only window in the room was so grimy only a little light got through. Flies were buzzing around the window, knocking against it with little pinging sounds. The desk was piled with papers and a crushed plastic water bottle and several rolls of blueprints lay on top of them. A bunch of metal rods leaned up against one corner of the room.

"Hello," I said. "I'm Janet Barkin."

"Matt Bauer," the man at the desk said. He was about fifty with short, tightly curled gray hair and thick gray eyebrows that stuck out from his forehead. Beneath them, hard dark eyes stared at me. He didn't smile or get up. I took a quick look around. No sign of Sink. When Bauer had agreed to meet with me, I had asked if Sink could be there too, but Bauer had not replied.

"Pleased to meet you, Mr. Bauer," I said politely. I looked for somewhere to sit, but there weren't any visitor chairs. So I stood.

"Well? What do you want? You got my letter. You got fifteen days to clear the premises."

"I didn't know you were my landlord," I said. "Our lease is with MB Properties."

"You don't have a lease," Bauer said. "You have a month-to-month deal and we have the right to give you fifteen days' notice. We just did. In writing. Registered."

"Are you MB Properties?" I asked.

"That's me. MB Properties. Bauer Construction. MaBa Leasing. Bauer Brothers Contractors. All me."

"Sounds like a pretty big operation," I said. "I didn't realize all those companies belonged to the same person."

"Most people don't," Bauer said. "I'm not one of those guys who needs to blow his own horn." He gave me a fierce look. "You've got fifteen days. And we keep your security deposit if the place isn't in the same condition as you found it. I heard you painted and put in new carpets. All that will have to come out. I want it like you found it." A fly buzzed over his desk, and he swatted at it. It buzzed back to the window.

"But it was a mess when we moved in. We fixed it up," I said.

"Leave it like you found it or we keep your security deposit," Bauer replied.

"Some guys totally trashed the place and smeared paint around," I said. "We had to repaint and replace the carpets. I'd think you'd appreciate it. It's much nicer now."

"Like you found it or we keep your security deposit," Bauer repeated, his expression even fiercer than before.

"You can't do that," I said. "And you have to give us thirty days. Fifteen is against the law."

Bauer sneered. "Been talking to your brother Dennis?"

"No, but . . ."

"I don't care what the law says. If you don't like it, sue me."

"How do you intend to make us leave? You can't. We have a right to stay."

"I heard you were a troublemaker," Bauer said. He leaned back, tilting his chair so it rested on its rear legs, and looked up at me. He had a hard face. His skin was tanned and leathery looking, his mouth a thin line, his neck thick and rigid as a tree trunk. "You better not make any trouble around here. You and your brother and those crazy lawsuits of his. Let him try one on me. I'm not afraid. I haven't done anything wrong and you can tell him I said so."

"But I don't . . ." I began.

"On day sixteen if you're not out, when you get to the office, you'll find your furniture on the street and your locks changed."

"The police . . ."

"I know you think you've got friends on the police. I heard about that. But it won't do you any good. I've got more friends than you have, I've got Alderman Synko and the city in my corner, so you better not take me on. I told your brother the same thing. You'll both regret it."

"I don't see why you are so angry. What have I ever done to you?"

"I have nothing more to say. On your way!" Bauer said. He had a command voice even more powerful than the one I used on Lech. It sent me walking toward the door, my legs moving before my mind caught up.

"But I wanted to ask about you and Alderman Synko," I said, turning away from the door and looking back at him. My voice came out high and weak.

"Alderman Synko and me, we're like this," Bauer said. He raised his hand and twisted his second and third fingers together. His forearm corded with muscle. I saw that his other fist was clenched. He was furiously angry but he was controlling it. "We know you women troublemakers are in this together, and we know your brother Dennis put you up to it because he hates Alderman Synko. We make things better in this town and your brother tries to suck us dry without putting anything back. Seems like you're the same. This city never had better friends than Alderman Synko and me. Don't think for a moment a bunch of losers and bimbos and punk kids with earrings in their eyebrows are anything to us."

A fly swooped toward him. Bauer grabbed at it, caught it, clenched it in his fist, and crushed it to death. He stared at me. Then he opened his hand and let the dead, crushed fly drop to the desk.

"This meeting is over," he said.

*   *   *

On my way back from Bauer's, I stopped to pick up some groceries for Mrs. Gretzky and burgers for me and Lech. I dropped the groceries off at Mrs. Gretzky's, filled her in on what had happened at Bauer's construction site, and got an earful from her about all the phone calls.

Then Lech and I went upstairs to my place. I fed Lech his burger and ate mine. It had gotten cold and grease had soaked through the bun. It tasted like Styrofoam. The fries were so soggy they could have been potato salad. The coleslaw left a sickly sweet taste of chemicals in my mouth. Disgusting. Even more disgusting, I ate every crumb and licked the box. And I wasn't really hungry. I was worried. Worried about the W.R.C., worried about Larry and me, and worried about Tiffany. I walked to the window and looked out.

It had grown dark, but the sky glowed a strange yellowy gray. If it hadn't been October, I would have said we were in for tornadoes. The dead-still quality of the air increased my nervousness. It felt like something bad was going to happen, which was weird, because plenty of bad things had already happened. What else could go wrong?

I called to Lech and we locked up and set off back to the W.R.C. office. We had scheduled an evening meeting to figure out what we were going to do about every agency in the city being after us. We had hoped I would find out something from Bauer and Sink, but Sink hadn't shown up and Bauer had been less than helpful.

I hadn't heard from Larry, but I hadn't expected to. No, that's a lie. I told myself he wouldn't call, but I kept hoping he would. I tried the trick of staring at my cell phone and willing it to ring, but no luck.

Face it, Janet, I told myself, *it's over. He has somebody new—Cheryl Spears—and he's just too kindhearted to tell you*. I made up my mind that no matter what, I would still try to help Cheryl Spears if she was in trouble because I owed it to Tod. Then, after the W.R.C. had solved her problem, I would pour a beer on her head. Or throw a pie in her face. Yes!

Just kidding.

Inside the W.R.C. office I found Porsha and Sally waiting for me.

"Mrs. Gretzky phoned," Sally said. "You forgot toilet paper. She wants to know if you can pick some up from the 7-Eleven on your way home. I told her you would."

I whopped my head with my hand. "I must be losing my marbles. She told me special not to forget it and then I did. For sure I'll stop on my way home." I thought how awful it must be to be dependent on other people for things like toilet paper. Mrs. Gretzky had been so independent until her legs went bad.

"So how did it go with Bauer?" Porsha asked.

"Not good," I replied. I recounted my conversation with Bauer, and I told them how he had repeated his threat to evict us, a threat we had already received in the mail.

"He told me that him and the city and Sink are tight," I said. "I think he was letting me know he and Sink are behind all the bad stuff that started happening to the W.R.C. all of a sudden."

"I can see it," Porsha said. "I bet they laid a lot of complaints and called in a lot of favors. Between them, they must have a ton of contacts with government people."

"All we need. Sink *and* Mr. Bauer after us," Sally said. "Seems like we sure know how to get the enemies."

"What I can't understand is how Mr. Bauer knows as much as he does," I said.

"What do you mean?" Sally asked.

"Like when he said, 'Don't think a bunch of losers and bimbos and punk kids with earrings in their eyebrows can get in our way.' How did he know?"

"How did he know what?" Sally said, looking puzzled.

"When Mr. Bauer said that about losers, bimbos, and punks, he meant the W.R.C., Tiffany, and Tod," Porsha explained. "Had to. You know there are people who think we're crazy here at the W.R.C. And people who think because Tiffany is blond and soft-spoken and easily frightened, she's a bimbo. And Tod—well, he definitely wears an earring in his eyebrow. The big question is, how did Bauer know about Tiffany and Tod?"

"I see what you mean," Sally said.

"And why did he think Dennis was behind everything?"

Porsha continued. "That was an odd thing to say. Why bring up Dennis?"

"He must have got that from Sink," I said. "Sink told me he believed Dennis was out to get him. If I were Sink, I would think that too, because Dennis holds grudges. Dennis remembers when he and Sink were both on the football team in high school, both stars. Now Dennis has a wrecked knee and is nobody special and Sink is a big man, and that makes Dennis mad."

"Mrs. Gretzky said she heard Sink is an investor in some of Bauer's companies and he got very rich from Mr. Bauer," Porsha told me. "Seems Bauer and Sink don't want anyone to know about it. But this old guy, who is a friend of Mrs. Gretzky's, worked at the office where they register who owns what. He saw the papers that prove Sink owns parts of Bauer's companies."

"Oh, boy," Sally said. "I wonder if Dennis knows. He'd be pretty jealous about Sink getting rich off Bauer while he has to fight for every scrap."

I agreed. I said, "I wonder if it's illegal—an alderman investing in property like that."

"I don't know," Porsha said. "But for sure, they are keeping it a secret. Even if it's legal, Sink has to know it would look bad if people found out."

"Bauer was real angry," I said. "Even though he didn't say it, I felt like he was threatening me all the time I was there. You should have seen him when he killed a fly that was bothering him."

"What do you mean?" Sally asked.

"The way Mr. Bauer looked at me when he did it—I felt like it was me he crushed in his hand."

Suddenly, Lech barked loudly, jumped up, and streaked toward the back of the office.

"What? Lech! What is it?" I shouted. I took off after him and Porsha and Sally followed me. I flung open the back door and Lech ran out into the alley, barking that loud, warning bark of his.

At the same time I heard a car zooming off down the alley. I caught a quick glimpse of it as it screeched away from us and around the corner, scraping against the wall. Its headlights were not on, so I saw only a dark blur as it vanished from sight.

Lech looked after it for a moment, then galloped over to something that lay at the place where the alley behind our office intersects the crossroad. He gave that terrible howl. The sound ran up my spine and chilled my heart.

We all ran toward him.

Beside Lech, lying under the beam of a security light, we saw the mangled body of a woman. Her body had been thrown off the crossroad and into our alley. From the way the blood had pooled in two places, it appeared she had been struck by the car, which flung her into the alley. Then she had been run over.

"A hit-and-run!" Sally cried.

I edged closer to the woman. I saw a leg wearing a big, thick-soled platform boot. I saw an outstretched arm. I saw a bloody T-shirt. Despite the blood, I could read the T-shirt. It said, "So Many Men, So Little Time." The body was bloody, mangled, twisted. And dead.

Then I saw the face. It was Tiffany.

CHAPTER 10

It was the afternoon after Tiffany's murder. Hard to believe it had been just last night we had found Tiffany in the alley and called 911. It seemed like a bad dream—the police coming, stringing up yellow tape around where Tiffany lay, setting up powerful lights, taking pictures, then questioning Porsha, Sally, and me about what we'd seen. And we had so little to tell them.

Since we'd stepped into the alley after Tiffany had been hit, none of us had gotten a good look at the car. None of us had seen a license plate. How could we convince the police Tiffany's death was no accident when it happened so fast and we hadn't actually seen it?

As soon as the police finished with us, I went home, walked Lech, and collapsed on my bed. I slept fitfully. Half-awake, half-asleep, I kept reliving the terrible events of the evening. In my imagination I heard Tiffany's frightened voice on the phone, I relived Lech's eerie mournful wail. I saw again the car careen off into the night. And printed on my mind, so I saw it every time I closed my eyes, was a picture of my friend's mangled body lying in a pool of blood.

Then this morning at the W.R.C. office, things were—if possible—worse than the day before. Official calls, threats, and warnings came in all day. The phone rang and people shouted at us. We hardly had time to swallow some sandwiches from the deli before the police called us to come in and sign our statements about the hit-and-run.

We went to the police station together, Sally, Porsha, and me. They were seen quickly. They signed their statements and were free to go.

But I was treated differently. After Sally and Porsha left to go back to the office, Larry called me into the interview room and asked me question after question. I could tell something was troubling him, and I could also see he wasn't going to tell me what it was. He was all business, acting so cold as if there were nothing between us and never had been.

As Larry questioned me, another policeman took notes, recording my every word. Behind Larry was the mirror I knew to be two-way glass. Other cops might be watching and listening, I told myself, so maybe that was why he was acting like we had never been close.

Finally Larry sighed, leaned back in his chair, and said, "You're sure that's all you can tell me?"

I nodded. My eyes burned with exhaustion and I felt as if bands of tension were tightening around my chest. I hated keeping things from Larry, but after all, he was keeping plenty from me.

He told the other cop we were done and we left the interview room, walked through the police station and out onto the street.

A fierce gust of wind blew in from the west. Grit and bits of trash swirled through the air and into our faces, and I could feel my eyes watering. We stood there in the wind, not speaking. Suddenly Larry said, "Janet?" and at the same time I said, "Larry?"

We looked at each other.

"What?" he said.

"I didn't say anything," I mumbled.

Larry leaned over and touched my cheek. He wiped away the tear that had seeped out of my eye, despite my trying my best to keep it in.

"Tiffany . . . I feel like it's my fault," I said.

We began walking along the street.

"You didn't kill her, Janet," he said gently. "You weren't at the wheel of the car that ran her down, so stop blaming yourself."

"That's not the point," I said. My throat was so clogged up, I could hardly speak. "Because of me, she's dead!"

"Why do you say that?" Larry asked, his voice soft. "You didn't do anything that led to her death, did you?"

"Of course not!" But I didn't look at him. I couldn't.

Because it was a lie. Tiffany's death was my fault.

My fault, because I had never taken her seriously with her crazy T-shirts and sexy clothes and the way she fell apart so easily. When Tiffany had told me she was scared to come to the W.R.C., I had reassured her everything would be okay. I told her to walk through dark streets alone at night and to come to the office, even though I knew she believed asking for the W.R.C.'s help put her in danger.

I had gotten Tiffany used to obeying my command voice, the same way I trained Lech. I had commanded

Tiffany to come to the office. She had obeyed—and now she was dead.

"Larry," I said, "you have to find out who did this to her."

"You're convinced it wasn't an accident, not just an ordinary hit-and-run?" Larry asked.

"Sure of it. She was scared. When she called me, she was afraid someone was listening as she spoke to me. She was afraid someone would find out she wanted our help. But I thought it was just Tiffany being her usual scaredy-cat self. I told her everything would be okay. Yeah. Right. Listen to Janet Barkin's advice and get yourself killed. Or, hey, sign up to work with Janet Barkin and watch the whole city come down on you like a ton of bricks. *And* maybe get killed as a bonus."

Larry stopped walking and turned to look at me. The wind blew my hair over my face and he reached out and brushed it away. "Janet, don't be so hard on yourself," he said.

But I barely heard his words. I saw the look in his eyes, and I felt myself melting as his fingers brushed across my face. "Larry," I said. The wind whipped the words away.

Larry leaned toward me, his hands pulling my face up to his.

Then he shook himself, dropped his hands, and started walking again. I stood there, puzzled, not understanding why he was acting the way he was.

He strode away from me and I speeded my steps to catch up to him.

"Larry . . ." I began.

"Why did you say the whole city is coming down on you?" Larry asked without looking at me.

I told him about all the officials who had suddenly

turned on us, all the notices and warnings the Women's Rescue Company had received. I told him about my meeting with Mr. Bauer and how he'd acted. "And I think it all goes back to Alderman Synko," I concluded. "Somehow, what's happening to the W.R.C. is connected with Barbara's death and Tiffany and the sexual harassment suit. I think someone wants to put us out of business before we get to the truth."

"That sounds like kind of a stretch to me," Larry said. "Why do you think Barbara's and Tiffany's deaths and the sexual harassment suit are linked?"

"How does it look to you, Larry?" I asked. "Do you think Barbara's being beaten to death was an accident and what happened to Tiffany an ordinary hit-and-run?"

"You know I can't answer that," Larry said. "The official story is that we are investigating." He turned toward me. "What aren't you telling me, Janet? What do you know that I don't?"

"What aren't *you* telling *me*?" I snapped back.

Suddenly, Larry grabbed my hand. "I've had enough of this," he said. "Come on."

Pulling me after him, he led me around the corner to his car, a dark blue 92 Ford Probe which he took care of almost as well as I looked after Lech. He pulled out a set of keys and opened the doors. "Get in," he said.

I got in.

"We've got to talk. I'm taking you to my place, okay?"

Although Larry and I had dated for several months, I had never seen his apartment. He had come up to mine several times, but he had never invited me to his place.

We drove southeast to the Hinman and Main area. Larry lived in an old, nicely maintained apartment building. It was U-shaped with a small fenced backyard.

Larry drove into an alley behind the building and then into a space in a six-stall garage. He parked and I followed him into the yard, up the back stairs, and onto his back porch.

Larry unlocked the back door and walked into the kitchen. I followed. He turned on the light. "Want a coffee?" he asked. Without waiting for my reply, he filled the kettle, took a bottle of instant out of the cupboard, pulled two mugs off a shelf, and spooned some coffee into each one.

The kitchen was old-fashioned with glass-fronted cupboards and a worn tile floor, but it was neat and bright. Through a doorway I could see the living room, so I walked in and looked around. Hanging on the walls, Larry had pictures of old-fashioned sailing ships. A faded red leather chair faced the television and here were floor-to-ceiling shelves holding an expensive-looking stereo set and a collection of hundreds of tapes and CDs. I walked over and checked them out. Larry had country, jazz, and even classical, but most of the tapes and CDs were Chicago blues bands. Other shelves held books—mostly history and biography, but one shelf displayed a collection of framed photos. In the center of all the photos was a large picture in an old-fashioned, silver frame. I moved in closer to look at it and I could hardly believe my eyes.

It was a picture of me.

Larry came up behind me and handed me a cup of coffee.

"I got that from the newspaper when they ran the article about you and the W.R.C. solving the murder on Lovers' Bridge," Larry said.

The picture showed me standing by a bridge. I was wearing a loose tunic top that somehow hid my extra pounds. A light breeze fluffed up my hair and the sun lit it from behind. I looked good in the picture.

"You are a beautiful woman, Janet," Larry said. I didn't turn to look at him. I sipped my coffee.

"I'm supposed to be dating Cheryl Spears," Larry said. "People need to think you and I have broken up. It's part of a case I'm working."

My heart lifted. If Larry said "broken up," that meant he thought we had been an item before. You don't break up with someone you were never involved with. Until this moment, I had been afraid that I was kidding myself about me and Larry. I wondered if I thought we were dating, but he thought we were just friends who flirted a little.

But seeing the picture there seemed to prove he cared for me. And it looked like he hadn't stopped caring, because the picture was front and center on his shelves, not stuck away in a drawer.

I did a quick scan to see if there were any pictures of Cheryl. Not a one.

"Can I ask why you are supposed to be dating Cheryl Spears?" I said.

"You can ask, but I can't answer," Larry replied. He stood close behind me. I felt his hand gently smooth my hair.

I slipped away from him, crossed the room, and sat in the armchair. He turned to watch me, leaning against the wall and sipping his coffee.

"I went to see Matt Bauer," I said, "and he warned me to back off investigating Barbara's death. He made it clear he and Sink want me to stop. He mentioned the W.R.C., Tiffany, and Tod Spears, Cheryl's brother. So I think whatever you're working on with Cheryl is part of what I'm involved in. Sooner or later you are going to have to trust me."

Larry sighed. He sat on the sofa and put his cup down

on his coffee table. "First, you need to tell me what you're hiding. You've been up to something."

"We've been around this before," I said. "You think you can keep things from me and I should spill everything I know to you? Forget about it."

"I'm the cop here!"

I just looked at him.

"It's your duty to tell me everything you know," Larry said.

"Duty! Why would I want to help you when you don't care who killed Barbara and Tiffany?"

Larry's blue eyes grew fierce. "I care," he said. "Count on it. If someone is responsible for their deaths, I'll get him."

I realized Larry meant it.

Then I thought, how could I have doubted him? I knew Larry too well to believe that he would let anyone, no matter how powerful, stop him from bringing a murderer to justice. How could I have thought Larry might be part of a cover-up? No wonder he wouldn't trust me, I hadn't trusted him. No, if Larry wasn't investigating, it was because he had good reason. Or maybe . . . he *was* investigating. Maybe he didn't want the fact of the investigation to get out, because it might put a suspect on guard.

"I guess it might be smart not to let anyone know you think Barbara was murdered," I said.

"I'll do whatever I have to do," Larry said.

"Okay," I said. "Here's something you should know. Tiffany and I went to Sink's office late at night. We were looking for some files Tiffany had taken out of Barbara's drawers and given to Sink. Files Dennis wanted to see and Sink wanted hidden from him."

"Janet!" Larry said.

I started to speak, but Larry held up his hand. "I would never tell you not to do what you think is right," he said, "but could you at least let me know when you're doing something dangerous?"

I felt like arguing, but I could tell from his face that Larry was upset and worried, so I said, "Okay, next time I do something dangerous, I'll give you a warning. Is that good enough?"

"Promise?" Larry said, looking at me with a look that held both concern and anger.

"I promise," I said. Then I continued, "We found out that Barbara had sexual harassment files on lots of people in that office. And even on people outside the office. While we were checking them out, someone broke into the office—a guy wearing a ski mask. I chased him away but he came back, trashed Sink's office, and stole some of the files. What if, when Sink found his trashed office and the missing files, he suspected Tiffany? He knew she had a key."

"Janet, you are amazing," Larry said, smiling at me. Then his face changed and he said, "But you shouldn't have done that."

I stretched out my hands. "Cuff me, officer, I admit to breaking and entering," I said, giving him a little smile.

He took my hands in his and held them. Then he pressed them to his cheek. "I don't think I'll arrest you just yet," he said, smiling back at me. "After all, you had a key, so it's not officially a break and enter." Then his smile faded. "Any idea who wrecked the office and took the files?"

"No. I think it was a man who was strong and fit. He pulled himself out of the window by his arms. Then he took off and Lech couldn't catch him. Maybe because he was a fast runner, or maybe because he went up the side of the building and over the roof. Not everyone could do that."

"Sink couldn't," Larry said.

"For sure," I said. "The guy wasn't as big and fat as Sink. And anyway, Sink already had the files. Why would he steal them from himself? But he must have suspected Tiffany when he found his office trashed and files stolen, because she had the keys."

"Did you see any of the files before they were stolen?"

"Just the labels on the folders. There were files on all the women at the office and some for Bauer Construction."

Larry shook his head in exasperation. "Cheryl claims there is no harassment at Bauer's."

"Is that right?" I said. "That's real interesting. Bauer acts like a man with something to hide. He's the W.R.C. landlord and he's evicting us. Not that it makes any difference. So many people are claiming the W.R.C. is in breach of some law or other, we are going to have to close down anyway."

"Close down the Women's Rescue Company?" Larry said. "That can't happen. You people do so much good in the neighborhood."

"Thank you," I said gratefully. Larry had been a supporter from day one, and his support meant a great deal to me. "But unless we can figure out who is behind this attack on us and stop them, I don't think we have much choice. I'd say we have about a week before the city shuts us down."

"I might be able to help you there," Larry said.

"Would you?" I asked him.

He was still holding my hands. Now he lifted them to his lips. I felt a thrill of pleasure as he kissed first the backs of my hands, then my palms. "Yes, I will."

"I'll help you too, Larry," I said. "I'll get to the bottom of this sexual harassment stuff. I'll find out what's going on at Bauer's and Alderman Synko's office."

"Sink isn't talking," Larry said. "At least, not to me."

"We'll see about that," I said.

CHAPTER
11

Although it was only six o'clock, dark had fallen. I had seen from the street that there was no one in the front office, so I went around the alley and there was Sink, working at his desk, his back to the window. The office was dark except for the desk light shining on a pile of papers. On the floor beside Sink's desk stood a paper shredder. He leafed through the files, from time to time selecting papers, which he fed into the shredder. Streams of paper like confetti came out of its sharp blades and fell into a wastebasket.

I knocked on the window. Sink swivelled in his chair and looked out into the alley, saw me, and opened the back door to his office. I came in, leaving Lech outside.

"Hey, how you doing, Janet," Sink said as I came through the door. But he did not say it with his usual good cheer.

"Fine," I said. My voice sounded gloomy too.

"Come on in, sit down. Is that your dog out there? Is he okay?"

"Yeah, he knows how to wait for me," I said. I sat in the chair opposite Sink's desk. The files I had seen him looking through a moment ago were gone. He must have shoved them into a desk drawer before he opened the door to let me in.

"Terrible about Tiffany, terrible," Sink said. "I can hardly believe it. Two tragedies, one right after another. And they say bad luck comes in threes."

For a moment I thought Sink looked scared. It was an unexpected look to see on the face of a man who was usually so jolly.

"I don't think luck had anything to do with what happened to Tiffany," I said. "Do you?"

Sink picked up a pen from his desk and scratched behind one ear with the round end. "Accident, bad luck, what else could it be? So what brings you here after hours?"

"Tiffany," I said. "She was scared of somebody, maybe someone in this office."

"Oh, Janet, let it be," Sink said.

I had never seen him like this. Sad. His voice flat. He was like a balloon with half the air let out.

"No, I won't let it be," I said. "She went out walking at night—you know she was scared to do that—because I told her it would be okay. I feel responsible."

Sink opened the top drawer of his desk, looked inside, then slammed it shut. He didn't say anything.

"Sink?" I said. "What was she frightened of? Was it you?"

"Me!" Sink said. His face got red. "I was crazy about her. I'd have done anything for her."

"She liked you too," I said.

"That's right," Sink said, looking at me eagerly. Then he blurted out, "We were in love."

"What?" I knew Sink was married. He had three grown-up children.

Sink smiled weakly. "You know what I mean. She was in love with me or—I don't know—she thought she was. Barbara told me it wasn't love. She warned me. Said it was just infatuation, that I shouldn't take advantage of a young girl. Then in her lawsuit, she called what was between Tiffany and me 'sexual harassment.' But Tiffany wouldn't go along with Barbara and Dennis and be part of their lawsuit. They tried to get her to, but she said no. She said she couldn't go against someone she was in love with."

"Love," I said. I remembered how Tiffany had talked about Sink. It *was* possible she thought she was in love with him. What a dim bulb. She worked in his office, she saw Sink hit on every woman who walked through the door, yet when he hit on her, she fell in love. It made you think there might really be some truth behind all those dumb blond jokes. Maybe if you were a blond, things came easier and you didn't have to learn to see the difference between real and pretend. But then I remembered how Tiff said that she had to choose to be either Sink's friend or his enemy. Sink made her choose and her job was at stake, so could I believe what Sink was telling me?

"Did she confide in you?" I asked Sink. "Tell you who she was afraid of?"

He picked up his pen and began doodling on a piece of paper. He drew a black cloud and then put crosses underneath it, making it look kind of like a cemetery. "We were only together two times," Sink said. "She wanted to see me again, but I came to my senses."

"Did others in the office know about you and her?" I asked.

The shrewd look came back into Sink's eyes. "I don't know for sure. But she didn't hide her feelings very well and people figure out what's going on in a small office like this."

"So you do think they knew?" I asked.

"The atmosphere around the office got tense. I'm a politician. I pick up on things . . . and I knew I had problems. We have enough jealousy and office politics here as it is—and the thing between Tiffany and me made it worse. It was a mistake . . ." He looked up at me, "I don't know why I told you about it. I'm not thinking straight. The way she got killed like that, run down in an alley, it really got to me."

He looked at me and held out his hands like he was praying. "Please, please, promise me you won't tell anyone about us, about Tiffany and me. She's dead now. We should respect her memory."

"So the atmosphere around the office got tense and you decided to end it with Tiffany, is that what you're saying?" I asked. "Your other staff were jealous, and they thought you were giving her too much attention?"

"I came to my senses," Sink repeated softly as if talking to himself. He dropped his hands onto the desk and stared at them like they belonged to someone else.

"How did she take you breaking up with her?" I asked, watching him. He looked so tired, so sad. He spoke as if he were giving me only half of his attention. As if his mind were somewhere else.

"Take what?" Sink asked. He drew a heart on his scrap of paper and then doodled a cross above it, so that it looked like the cross stabbed into the heart.

"Sink!" I said. "Tiffany is dead. Maybe someone on your staff was jealous, thought the affair was dangerous to you as a politician. Maybe they thought Tiffany would tell about the affair, make it public, side with Barbara in the suit, cause you trouble."

"No, no, no, that's crazy," Sink said. His eyes narrowed. "People say you are a troublemaker." His voice had changed. It was harder somehow, meaner. "I never saw it. But now I'm starting to wonder. What are you up to? You trying to get people to suspect me of doing her harm? Why do you say these things?"

"I was just wondering . . ."

"You better not tell the cops what you were 'just wondering.' Do you understand me?"

He was about to kick me out of the office. I could see it in his eyes. "I . . ." I took a deep breath, gagged, and coughed. I gasped for breath and coughed harder.

Sink jumped up from his desk, rushed around behind me, and whacked me on the back. "Janet! Are you okay?"

"Water . . ." I gasped.

He hurried out of the office, and I could hear him run through the hall and into the front office where the water cooler was. I heard water gurgling.

Quick as a flash I darted around to the front of his desk. I pulled open the top drawer and ran my eyes over the files. Then I saw a key ring. It was Tiffany's, the one she had handed to me to open the office door. I grabbed it and stuck it into my pocket.

Hearing Sink's footsteps coming back, I zoomed back around the desk and regained my seat.

Sink bustled back in, holding a coffee mug. "Here, it's water, take a sip," he said.

I grabbed the water, coughing hard, spilling a little,

gasping, and swallowed some down. I choked noisily, coughed again, then drank the rest. "Thanks," I said, between coughs. I swallowed the remaining water and handed the mug to him.

He looked down at me, his face full of concern. "Better? Do you need any more?"

"No, thanks, that did the trick." I wiped my chin where the water had dribbled down. Then I stood up. "I better be going," I said.

Sink studied my face. "Those crazy ideas of yours, you're not going to go spreading them around, are you?"

"Of course not," I said, giving him my biggest smile.

He smiled back, but his smile looked forced. He opened the back door for me.

I stepped outside and signaled to Lech.

"Janet, are you up to something?" he called after me as I set off down the alley.

"Me?" I turned to look at him. I couldn't see his face as he stood in the dark, shadowy doorway. "You don't need to worry about *me.*"

He didn't reply, but I had the feeling he wasn't smiling any longer.

*   *   *

Using Tiffany's key I opened the door to her building and took the elevator up. As it ascended, I reflected. I remembered the moment I'd looked in Sink's desk drawer. I'd hoped to find out what files he'd wanted to shred, but instead I'd caught sight of Tiff's keys. At once, I'd decided to check out her apartment, see if I could find any clues to what she had been so afraid of.

But now that I was in her building, it didn't seem like quite such a good idea.

The hall outside her door was littered with flyers for take-out food. The greasy, stained walls were thin, and I could hear babies crying and radios blaring and smell food cooking.

Inside her apartment, I turned on the lights and gave the place a quick once-over to be sure no one was there. I told Lech to sit by the front door and stand guard, but even with him there, I felt nervous and uneasy.

Tiffany's apartment was a tiny, dark efficiency, one large room with a kitchen area at one end and a futon bed at the other. There was a table by the window covered with a pink-checked cloth. In the center was a makeup mirror surrounded by jars and bottles of cosmetics. Among them sat a cup of coffee with a skin of greenish-white mold on top.

Aside from the futon and the table, Tiffany didn't have much furniture—just a chest of drawers and an old chair, looking like thrift-store bargains or parents' hand-me-downs.

Clothes were thrown about and the place smelled like stale perfume and rotting food. That smell might have been coming from soggy-looking pizza boxes sticking out of the wastebasket. There were dirty dishes in the sink and stacks of *Cosmopolitan* magazines on top of the fridge.

Stuffed animals—three teddy bears, a Cabbage Patch doll, and a large ratty-looking Garfield—were scattered over the bed. Papers and file folders lay among them.

Lech sat watching me restlessly, his tail twitching, his body tense, so I told him he didn't have to guard anymore. Immediately, he paced around the room. He sniffed at the pizza boxes in the garbage and tried to stick his nose under the futon bed, but the bed was just a pad on the floor, so he had no luck.

"I won't be long, Lech," I told him.

I looked through the papers on the bed while Lech kept trying to push his nose under the futon.

"Something under there?" I asked him. I slipped my hand between the futon and the floor. My fingers touched something and I pulled out a small book.

I turned it over in my hands. It was bound in pink quilted leather and held shut with a strap secured by a tiny gold lock. I checked Tiffany's key ring, found a key that looked right, and tried it. The little lock opened.

The book was Tiffany's private diary, filled with her large, childlike handwriting in ink of different colors—purple in places, green in others, bright pink in others. Sprinkled here and there Tiffany had drawn hearts and smiley faces. Some of the smiley faces smiled, but others frowned and a few had teardrops dripping from them.

For a moment, I hesitated. It felt very wrong to read Tiffany's diary—to intrude upon her privacy. In a way the whole apartment was like Tiffany's diary. It was a side of her I did not think she would want anyone to see. If she were expecting visitors, she would clean it up, put away the makeup, and hide the diary, the files she had taken, and the stuffed animals. She wouldn't want anyone to know she had taken files from Sink's office. And even more, she would hate a friend or a lover knowing that she needed teddy bears to keep from being scared at night and that her life was so out of control.

I wish I hadn't seen this secret side of Tiffany.

But I had. And if I were going to avenge her death, I needed to read her diary, I needed to know what she knew and what she was afraid of.

I curled up on the bed and started to read.

The phone rang.

Without thinking, I reached over the side of the bed

and picked it up. "Hello?" I said.

"Who . . . ?" a man's voice said.

I didn't answer. I held the phone to my ear, waiting to see if the man would say more, trying to figure out who could be calling Tiffany. Surely all her friends knew she was dead by now. Then I thought, what if someone was watching her apartment building? What if they knew which was her apartment and saw the light go on? What if they called on a cell phone to see if they could recognize the voice of the person inside, if that person were dumb enough to pick up the phone? As I thought this, the person on the other end of the phone line hung up.

"Lech, we better get out of here," I said. "Now."

I scooped the papers off the bed, jammed them and Tiffany's diary into my backpack, turned off the lights, and locked the door, and Lech and I headed for the elevators.

Standing in the hall, waiting for the elevator, I watched the indicators. One elevator was on the main floor. Now it was coming up and I watched as the indicator showed it mounting the floors: two, three, four . . . I was on the sixth floor.

What if the person who had called me was on the way up? It could be a cop. Larry. Did I want to tell Larry I had taken stuff from Tiffany's apartment? I'd have to think about that.

Or what if it was Tiffany's murderer?

Whoever it was, one thing was for sure. I didn't want anyone to find me standing here with Tiffany's files and diary in my knapsack.

Lech and I ran down the hall to the exit door. We pushed it open.

Down the stairs we went.

The stairs ended in a tiny hallway with only one door. I opened it a crack and looked out into the lobby. I didn't see anyone. I glanced over to the elevators. Above them was the lighted display that told which floor each elevator was on. I saw that one was in the parking lot basement. The other was stopped at the sixth floor.

Lech and I tore through the lobby and out onto the street.

If anyone looked down from Tiffany's apartment, they might see us running away, but I didn't care. I was spooked.

Someone had called Tiffany's place, heard my voice, then—maybe—headed up to her apartment.

If someone feared what Tiffany knew and killed her because of that, now they might think I knew it too.

CHAPTER 12

When the alarm went off the next morning, I opened my eyes to a strange darkness. I got up and looked out the window. The sky was dark with pale greenish-yellow streaks of light in the thick cloud cover. I slid open the window. The air felt clammy and heavy and although it had not rained, the tires of the cars below made moist sounds as they drove by.

Lech had been sleeping by my bed. He trotted over to the window, put his paws on the sill, and peered out, sniffing.

"Feels like tornado weather, doesn't it?" I said to him. "But not in October, right?"

I made myself some instant coffee. I hadn't had time to go shopping and couldn't find anything to eat except a stale Mars bar so it would have to do.

As Lech and I approached the W.R.C. office, we heard the loud roar of construction machinery. Traffic was backed up on Dempster, and ahead of me I could see that the sidewalk was barricaded. Then I saw a big yellow front-end loader with a backhoe attached tearing up the parking lot in front of the W.R.C. office. The sidewalk in front of our door had turned into a crumbling hole, and slabs of broken asphalt had been piled so it was impossible to get anywhere near our office. The doughnut shop to the right of us and the dry cleaner to the left were also cut off. As I watched, a dump trunk with "Bauer Construction" written on the side drove up and parked, and the front-end loader began dumping chunks of asphalt into the truck. Huge clouds of dust billowed into the air and the tumbling masonry sounded like a house collapsing.

A guy in a hard hat and orange reflector vest was standing by the sidewalk barricade.

"Hey, what's going on?" I shouted to him above the noise of machinery and junk clattering into the dump truck.

"Ripping up the parking lot!" he shouted back.

"Why?" I screamed. "What was wrong with it?"

He shrugged and made a gesture with his hands that meant: "How should I know? It's nothing to do with me. I just work here."

"How are we supposed to get into our office?" I yelled.

The guy shrugged again.

"Come on, Lech," I said. "Let's go around through the back."

Pursued by dust and noise, we retraced our steps to the corner, turned, and went down the alley behind our strip mall. We both slowed at the place where Tiffany had been struck down. A fine scatter of glass glittered here and there, and you could still see the bloodstains on the pavement.

I opened the back door with my key and went into the

office. Sally and Porsha were already there. They were standing at the front window, watching the backhoe rip up the parking lot. I joined them.

"Hey, Janet," Porsha said. "Look at what Matt Bauer's got going out there."

"Yeah, I saw," I said.

"It's a vendetta. That man wants to cause maximum pain," Porsha said, her eyes following the bucket of the front-end loader.

The bucket rose higher and higher and then dumped its load, and because the chunks of asphalt and stones fell from such a height, they made a terrible racket. Even inside, the noise was deafening. Our front window was covered with grit.

"What's a vendetta when it's at home?" I asked Porsha.

"A feud, a fight to the death," Porsha replied.

Sally sighed. She was all dressed up to go to the hair salon. She wore her short blond hair straight and hanging over one eye, narrow black pants, and a T-shirt that was so short you could see a strip of skin between it and her pants. "Look at my shoes," she said.

I saw that her black lace-up combat boots were covered with dirt.

"Mr. Bauer isn't going to give up," Sally said. "And what can we do? If he leaves the front of the office all ripped up like that, no clients are going to be able to get in."

I took some paper out of my drawer, found a magic marker, and started to scribble. "We'll make signs telling people to come in through the alley and put them up on the corners," I said.

"Janet," Sally said, "everybody's mad at us. The doughnut store and the dry cleaner know Mr. Bauer is doing this because we won't vacate like he wants us to.

They say we're wrecking their business. A few signs aren't going to cut it."

"Too bad," I said, making a big black arrow on my sign. It reminded me of the crosses Sink had made when he doodled. And that reminded me of what I had seen in his office and found at Tiffany's.

"Wait till you guys hear what happened when I went to see Sink last night," I said.

I filled them in.

As I spoke, Sally got more and more upset. "Oh, God, you're turning into a break-and-enter artist, Janet," she said. "What if the person who called you at Tiffany's apartment is her killer? Do you think he figured out you were there? Is he after you?"

Porsha didn't wait for my answer. "Hey, Janet, that's cool," she said. "What did you find in the files and the diary? Tell us, come on, the suspense is killing me." She looked at her watch. "And tell quick 'cause I've got to be at school in half an hour."

Before I could reply, someone banged on the back door. I looked at Lech. He was calm, so I went to open it.

It was Tod Spears.

"Hi, Tod," I said. "Come on in."

Tod gave me a dirty look and stalked in. He was wearing baggy pants, his flashy Nike sneakers, and a grey, hooded sweatshirt and carrying a skateboard under his arm. He dropped the skateboard with a clatter and collapsed onto a chair. "Thanks a lot!" he said, glaring at me.

"Now what?" I said to him. "What's got you in such a bad mood?"

"I trusted you, that's a laugh," Tod said. "I shoulda got my head drilled instead."

Porsha, Sally, and I looked at each other. Porsha went over and knelt down in front of Tod's chair. "Hey, man, what's the matter? You can trust Janet. She's, like, the most honorable person in the neighborhood. Count on it."

"That's what *you* say. That's what everybody says. But they say wrong!" Tod shouted.

"Why do you think that?" Sally asked in her gentlest, sweetest, kindest voice.

Tod looked at her admiringly. I had forgotten what an impression she made on him the first time he saw her.

Sally brushed her blond hair out of her eye and smiled at Tod.

He blushed. "She, like, got her brother on Cheryl's case and now things are worse than ever at Cheryl's job. And Cheryl says it's all my fault."

"You mean Dennis?" I said, astonished. "Dennis is hassling Cheryl?"

"Like, pretend you're surprised," Tod said.

"Jeez, I *am* surprised," I said. "I never talked to Dennis about Cheryl. The last time I saw him he practically threw me out of his apartment. My brother and I don't get along."

"Yeah, sure. Give me a break," Tod said.

"If she says so, it's true," Porsha said.

"You can trust Janet," Sally said.

Tod's shoulders slumped and he seemed to wilt in his chair. "Well, like, whatever," he mumbled. Then he said, "But if you didn't sic your brother on Cheryl, what's happening?"

I sat at my desk while Porsha and Sally pulled up chairs to sit near Tod. "Why don't you tell me what's going on," I said to Tod.

"Like, how would *I* know?" Tod cried. "I came here to find out!"

All three of us looked at him.

"It's getting worse," he said. "I heard Cheryl talking to a guy on the phone, like, arguing with him, you know? She saw me listening and made me leave. So, like, I went into the bedroom, but I left the door open a crack? And I heard her say she wouldn't do it, it would get her fired. Then he said something and she said she didn't believe him. Then he said something and she looked like she was going to cry. She told him he had her between a rock and a hard place, whatever that means."

"Why do you think it was Dennis she was talking to?" I said.

"Because when she hung up, she was really toasted and I, like, asked her, who that was on the phone. And she said it was, like, this slimebucket lawyer, Dennis O'Hara. She was real mad. She said he was the kind of guy who promises you diamonds and then gives you a lump of dirt, and no way was she going to fall for it."

"Do you know what she meant?" I asked.

"No, but, like, you tell me why this cop and now this lawyer are on my sister's case. What's she ever done to deserve this? She just wants to keep her job. All right?"

"The cop," I said. "Is that Larry Keegan?"

"That's the guy," Tod said. "You know him?"

Sally, Porsha, and I looked at each other.

"You say Larry's hassling your sister?" I asked Tod. "Are you sure?"

"No, I'm not sure. Someone told me they had a thing going, and when I asked Cheryl she said, like, no way. So I couldn't figure it out? That's why I hired you guys, okay?"

"Tod," I said, "listen to me. We said we'd help and we will. I'm going to call Larry Keegan and tell him what you told me. We'll find out what's going on, one way or another."

"Like, he's going to tell you?"

"Yes," I said. "He and I are working this together."

I saw Porsha and Sally look at one another in surprise.

"So just hang in there for another day or two," I said to Tod.

Tod looked out the window. The front-end loader was very close. It raised up its giant bucket with the huge pointed metal teeth, tilted it, and dumped a load of dirt and rocks right in front of our office. I saw that while we had been talking to Tod, the loader had created a pile of rubble in front of the office that was almost as high as the window.

"Wow, look at that!" Tod said. "Looks like you guys got your own troubles. Nobody will be able to get in to see you. You could be walled up in here like that movie, you know, where they bury the guy alive?"

I smiled reassuringly at Tod. "It's all under control," I lied. "Don't worry about it."

"Yeah. Right. Whatever," Tod said.

Tod left and Porsha followed him. She needed to get to school. As soon as they were gone, I called Larry and told him everything Tod had told me.

"Damn!" Larry said. "Cheryl's supposed to say we're dating. She promised. Do you think Tod has told other people that we're not?"

"Tod is only a kid," I said. "He's frightened for his sister. If she loses her job, he'll have to go back to living in foster homes. He sees his life falling apart."

"She promised not to say anything," Larry said. "For her own protection, we have to keep Bauer off guard. If he finds out Cheryl is helping me, things could get really messy."

"Whatever you and Cheryl are doing, I don't think it's working, because from what Tod said, it looks like Cheryl is close to getting fired. And now my brother is hassling her too."

"I know all about that," Larry said. "Don't worry about it."

"What? Don't worry that my brother and you are about to make a woman lose her job?"

"It will be okay," Larry said.

Something in his voice made me doubt him.

"Did you talk to Sink about Tiffany?" Larry asked.

"Yes. I checked out her apartment too. I didn't see any signs that you guys had been there."

"You went to her apartment?" Larry said. I could tell he was upset. "We can't do that without a warrant signed by a judge. We need a good reason—probable cause—to search someone's private space."

"Luckily, I'm not a cop," I said.

"What did you find?"

I hesitated. I wasn't thrilled with myself, reading Tiffany's diary and the files she had taken. Telling Larry what I had found out felt sleazy too. But hadn't Larry and I agreed to work together? "I found files Tiff took from Sink's office," I said. "And her diary. Together with what Sink told me, I have stuff you need to know. And another problem—it's possible someone saw me go in there. I had a bad feeling when I left, like someone was following me. Would that have been you or another cop?"

"No," Larry said. "I don't like the sound of that. I'm coming over."

"You can't get in from the front," I said, looking toward the window. It was now completely blocked by a huge dirt-and-rock mountain. At the very top of the pile, the teeth of the front-end loader looked like sharp knives as they tilted down, pouring out the dirt. One good thing— the dirt mountain seemed to mute the noise of the loader and rat-a-tat of the pneumatic drills breaking up the sidewalk.

"Why not?" Larry asked.

"Bauer's sent a lot of heavy machinery to rip up the parking lot. They've blocked the front of our office. Drive down the alley and knock on our back door. I haven't told Sally and Porsha what I found out in Tiffany's apartment, so as soon as you get here, I'll fill you all in."

"Whatever you do, don't leave the W.R.C. office," Larry said. "It's not safe. Hang in there, Janet. I'm on my way."

CHAPTER 13

I heard Larry knock and I opened the door. He came in without a word and sat on the chair next to my desk.

"What's the matter?" I asked. "You look upset."

"You've made a lot of people really mad, Janet," Larry said. "I've been checking around to find out why the city is after you, why Bauer wants to evict you."

"So what did you find out?" I asked. Sally, who had been sitting at her desk, came over and settled into a chair near Larry, so she wouldn't miss a word.

Larry said, "What I hear on the street is that you and your brother Dennis are out to destroy Alderman Synko and Matt Bauer."

I shrugged my shoulders. People could say what they wanted. The W.R.C. was determined to find out who killed Barbara and Tiffany and let the chips fall where they may.

"Janet," Larry said, "you act like you don't care, but you should. Bauer is one of the biggest employers in this city."

"So?" I said. But I saw how serious Larry looked and I realized he was telling me something I had to listen to. I couldn't ignore the fact that Bauer and Sink were influential men, and I couldn't ignore how much good they did, either. They made jobs, helped many people, and the neighborhood was behind them. Hadn't Bauer found a job for Mrs. Gretzky's useless nephew and given Cheryl a job when no one else would? And another thing, nobody thought Sink and Bauer were crooks. Okay, maybe they didn't follow every bend and twist of the law, but our town would be a worse place if they were brought down.

"You've made some powerful enemies," Larry said to me. "The threats to take away your license to operate, to cite you for breach of bylaws, the construction outside, your eviction notice—Sink and Bauer made all that happen."

"Sink never said anything about causing us trouble when I saw him," I replied. "He acted like we were friends."

"A man like Sink can smile and step on you at the same time," Larry said. "He likes you, but he has to protect the neighborhood, or that's how he sees it anyway. To him, you're just a girl with a hobby—the W.R.C.—and he figures if he makes it rough for you, you'll go away and let him get on with being the best alderman in town."

"That's a load of crap!" I shouted. I jumped up from my desk, stomped over to the file cabinet, opened a drawer, and banged it shut with the loudest bang I could make. The whole file cabinet shook.

"Of course it is," Larry said, smiling for the first time since he'd entered the office. "Come on, sit down, let's think this through."

I walked back to my desk and sat down.

"Sink is spreading the word that Dennis and the W.R.C. are causing trouble in the neighborhood and putting jobs at risk," Larry continued. "He is sure you and your brother are working together and other people think so too. Now it's your turn. What have you found out?"

But I was still steaming. "Let's get one thing clear," I said. "The W.R.C. is serious and we are here to stay. And I am *not* working with Dennis and I don't trust him anymore. The more I find out about him, the more I realize how much he's changed since we were kids."

Larry gave me a look like he wasn't sure whether to believe me. Maybe Larry loved his own brothers and sisters and could not imagine how Dennis and I had grown apart since his accident.

"You asked what I found at Tiffany's," I said to Larry. "Do you want to see the stuff I took?" I hoped Larry would take Tiffany's papers off my hands, because I had the feeling someone knew I had taken them and would try to get them back from me. It would be nice to be able to say I gave them to a cop.

"I have no legal right to see them," Larry said, "but you could tell me what they say."

"Dennis and Barbara were working together," I replied. "Barbara was pressuring Tiffany to join her suit for sexual harassment. The papers I found at Tiffany's were copies of statements by both Barbara and Tiffany. The statements claimed Sink sexually harassed Tiffany. But here's the interesting thing. Barbara's statements were signed but Tiffany's weren't."

"What does that mean?" Sally asked.

"I'm not sure. When I talked to Sink, he told me Barbara wanted Tiffany to join her suit, but Tiff refused. Because of what I read in the diary, I think it's more complicated."

"Complicated?" Sally said. "Like how?"

"You'd need to see it through Tiffany's eyes to understand," I said. My backpack was under my desk. I pulled it out and retrieved Tiffany's diary. Larry looked at it longingly, and I thought sooner or later, he'd give in and read all her papers. How could he resist?

I thumbed through the diary. "Tiffany believed she and Sink were in love," I said. "Then things went bad between them. Listen to this:

'Friday, Sept. 18

'Tonight Sink told me he loves me. I love him too. Mrs. Tiffany Synko. I feel like writing those words a thousand times. They sound so beautiful. Like they were meant to be. Everybody in the office will be so amazed!!!! I wonder how long a divorce takes? He looked so happy when I told him how I feel. But why did he get so sad all of a sudden? I don't understand.'"

"Poor Tiffany," Sally sighed. "Could she really have thought Sink would divorce his wife for her? It's so sad."

It was more than sad. Sink had taken advantage of Tiffany, a person who was easy to influence and anxious to please. It wasn't right.

I turned some pages. "A few days later she wrote this," I said.

"'Thursday, Sept. 24

'Sink stinks. From now on, I'm calling him Stinko. Ucky disgusting man!!!! I hate hate hate him!!!!! Barbara was right!!!! He was just using me. He must have just wanted sex with me because now he says he doesn't love me, it was a mistake and we should put it behind us. Can you believe that, Diary? Last night I cried all night, so hard my pillow was soaked with tears. Dear Diary, my heart is broken and I will never love again.

Barbara wants me to join her lawsuit against Stinko. Before, when she told me about the lawsuit, I thought she was jealous of our love, but now I wonder. Could he have done the same thing with her he did to me? Barbara and Dennis say I can take Sink for a lot of money and make a fool of him the way he made a fool of me. Maybe he will even lose the next election if word gets out how he broke the heart of a girl who works in his office.

Dennis says Sink used and abused me and I have to stop him before he does it to anyone else, that it's my duty. I am so torn, Dear Diary, I don't know what to do. When I think of his soft blue eyes and sweet words I can't bear to hurt him, but he broke my heart and I have to be strong and make him sorry he treated me like that. But if I sue him, will I lose him forever?'"

Here the diary was stained with tears and the little ink drawings of broken hearts and sad faces had run into one another to create a smudgy mess.

"Tiffany read too many romance novels," Sally said. "Sometimes I think those things ought to be banned."

"There's more, pages and pages more about her broken heart," I said, "but you get the idea. It seems like, at first, she refused to join Barbara and Dennis's suit against Sink because she thought they were in love, but when Sink broke her heart, she considered going along to get back at him. The papers on her bed were statements claiming Sink had harassed her, but she hadn't signed them. Maybe she couldn't decide what to do and that's what she was coming to see me about."

"Is there anything in the diary or the papers that gives us a lead on who might have wanted to kill her?" Larry asked.

"I was getting to that," I said. "There's one entry." I

opened the diary again and turned the pages until I got to the one I wanted. I read:

> "'Friday, Oct. 2
>
> 'Everyone is using me for their own selfish reasons. Barbara. Sink. Dennis. Matt. They try to get me to do things and I believe them and then it turns out they are lying. They don't care about me or my feelings. I could be dead for all they care!!!! What if I told what I know? I could tell Janet. I trust her. Janet is strong and brave and sincere. Janet will know what to do.'"

I felt my throat clog, and tears pressed against my eyes. I blinked, cleared my throat and continued to read.

> "'Lies! Lies! Lies! I'll expose them. Everyone thinks the truth is one thing. But I know it's the opposite. I'll tell. I promised not to, but a promise made to a liar doesn't count. I hate them all! They'll be sorry they treated me like dirt!!!!!!!! People can threaten to hurt me, but I don't care. I'll make them sorry they treated me so bad, if it's the last thing I do.'"

I stopped reading and closed the diary. "That's the final entry," I said.

"Any clues as to who she was talking about?" Larry asked. "Who was threatening her?"

"No. It could be Sink. But it could be Dennis or Bauer too."

"Bauer?" Larry said. "How does he come into it?"

"I don't know," I said. "But that section I read you earlier, where she lists the people who she says are using her, he's on that list."

"Let's get Cheryl over here," Larry said. "I want her to

hear that diary. If we put Tiff's problems together with what's happening to Cheryl, we might be able to figure out what's going on."

"She's helping you investigate something at Bauer's, right?" I asked.

Larry picked up the phone and keyed in a number. He spoke briefly, then hung up. "Cheryl goes on lunch break in ten minutes. She'll come over then," he said.

While we waited for Cheryl, Larry gave in to temptation and looked through the papers and diary I had taken from Tiffany's apartment. When he had finished, he said he didn't get any more from them than I had, but he'd like to read them again. I agreed.

Cheryl came in through the back door. Larry introduced everybody, we all shook hands, and I got her a coffee and a doughnut.

Cheryl was as pretty as I remembered. She wore a white T-shirt, a Cubs baseball jacket, faded jeans, and sneakers. She looked very strong with her wide shoulders, straight posture, and a way of walking that told you she was athletic. When I invited her to take a seat, she grabbed a heavy old oak chair from the corner with one hand, lifting it up like it weighed an ounce, and set it down by my desk.

"You lift weights or something?" I asked her.

"I work out," Cheryl said. She sat down and put her fists on her knees. She looked tense, like she thought someone might be about to attack her and she wanted to be ready to strike back.

"That's great," I said. "I want to do that. Is it hard to start when you've never done it?"

Cheryl's face softened and she smiled at me. "No, it's easy. I could take you to the Y where I work out and get you started."

"Would you?"

"Sure," Cheryl replied. "Larry says you have a lot of determination and you stick with things. I bet you'd be good at it."

We smiled at one another. Even though I hadn't meant to, I liked Cheryl. Of course, it helped that I knew she and Larry weren't involved, but she had a warm, open smile and a way of speaking that seemed completely honest. Nothing phony about Cheryl.

"Cheryl, tell Janet and Sally what's been going on at Bauer's," Larry said.

"I thought you wanted it to be a secret," Cheryl said, looking puzzled.

"The W.R.C. is going to help us," Larry said. "We need to take them into our confidence."

Cheryl hesitated, looked at me as if trying to decide if she could trust me. Then she said, "Okay, if Larry says it's all right." She glanced at Larry, who nodded, and she went on, "A little while ago I started getting anonymous letters. They said if I didn't cooperate, they'd make trouble for me at Bauer's. About the same time, Bauer found out someone was stealing stuff off construction sites. He's been trying to find out who is doing it, but so far, no luck. Everyone who works there and knows the work schedules and has keys is under suspicion, including me. I didn't do it, but with my record . . ."

We all got the point. With her record, she'd be a natural suspect.

"What did the anonymous letters mean by 'cooperate'?" Sally asked.

"They wanted me to sue Bauer for sexual harassment," Cheryl said. "I was supposed to work with Janet's brother Dennis, claim a huge settlement, then give

Dennis half. Barbara Noyes came around and offered to help me, but I figured that she was working with Dennis—and she'd probably skim off the rest of any money I got if I went along."

"Matt Bauer called the police to report the thefts," Larry said. "I went around to see him and to interview some of the staff."

I looked at Larry when he said this, because as far as I knew, Larry worked homicide. He avoided my eyes and kept talking.

"Cheryl showed me the anonymous letters and we decided to work together to find out what was going on—who was behind the thefts and who was sending the letters."

"The letters said if I called the cops, they would hurt Tod," Cheryl continued. She jumped up and strode around the office. "That's why Larry and I pretended we were dating. If we were seen together, people would think that was why, and no one would know I had gone against what the letters said and told the cops everything. I hope it didn't cause you any problems, Janet. Larry told me that you and he would go into a holding pattern until this was over."

"Oh, no, no bother at all," I said.

"I'm not quite getting this," Sally said. "Was Bauer harassing you or harassing other women? Did Barbara and Dennis think you had good reason to sue him?"

"You ever worked at a construction company?" Cheryl asked.

"No," Sally replied.

"Well," Cheryl said, smiling, "let's just say guys have a way of acting when they put on steel-toed boots and hard hats. Just like they have a way of acting when they're with their buddies drinking beer in a bar, and it's not the same way they'd act at their daughter's wedding."

I didn't agree with Cheryl, but I didn't say anything.

Cheryl continued, "About a week before I got the first anonymous letter, Dennis came around to the site. He invited me out to lunch. I didn't know why he invited me, but I figured what did I have to lose? I forgot there is no such thing as a free lunch. If I had realized why he asked me, I never would have gone, because I think Bauer saw us together and got the wrong idea."

"What did Dennis want?" I asked.

"He asked me a lot of questions about what it was like for me, as a woman, working at Bauer's. I said it was great."

"Then he asked me if any of the men made remarks about my body and asked for sex and kept on asking if I said no. I told him sure they did. But they didn't mean any harm. Most of them, anyway. And the ones who got obnoxious, well, I could handle it. No big deal."

Sally and I looked at one another.

"He asked me if Bauer's had a policy on sexual harassment, if they had anyone I could complain to. I just laughed. Then he said I could sue, get big bucks. I said, 'Why would I want to do that? I'm making decent money. Bauer's took me on when no one else would. I need the job. My brother is counting on me.' I told Dennis, no way would I sue Bauer's."

"Why not?" Sally said. "It sounds like there was good money in it."

"Get real," Cheryl said. "Everybody knows lawsuits go on forever. The lawyers make out like bandits and everyone else gets screwed. People like me end up out of a job while the lawyer is laughing all the way to the bank."

"Did you tell Dennis you thought that?" Sally asked.

"Sure. Why not? It's the truth and what could he say? Was he going to promise me I'd end up better off? He told me about lots of women who'd got big money working with him, but it sounded like a crock to me. So I told him, no way. He saw I meant it, we shook hands, he went away, and I forgot about the whole thing. But then Bauer found out about the thefts and the anonymous letters started coming."

"Dennis is running a scam," I said slowly as I figured it out. "Maybe Barbara was his partner. Barbara finds women she thinks are vulnerable, and Dennis and Barbara pressure them into suing their employers for sexual harassment. Then Dennis and Barbara get a big chunk of money, either from the lawsuit or maybe from the employers who pay them to drop the suit and go away—which is what Sink planned to do. They pressured Tiffany. They pressured you. It's mostly about money. Dennis doesn't care if there's real sexual harassment or not—I'm sure of that. I know my brother. And I bet he gets a big thrill out of humiliating men who are successful, men like Alderman Synko and Matt Bauer. It makes me so mad. Sexual harassment is a real problem, and people like Dennis make things worse, not better."

"I think you're right," Larry said.

"It fits with how Dennis acted about the lawsuit idea," Cheryl said. "But do you think your brother could be behind the anonymous letters?"

"It's the kind of sneaky thing I can see him doing," I said sadly. "But even if he wanted to steal from Bauer— and I don't see it—how could he? You say it has to be someone who knows the work schedules and has access to the keys? That doesn't fit Dennis."

"Right. We put up temporary huts at most of our construction sites, and we lock them. The keys to the huts are kept in my office in a lockbox. I have access to that box, and Bauer does, and a few of the senior guys do. Before the thefts started, we were kind of careless about the key box, but once we realized what was going on, we changed the lock and now only four people have access to that box. But the thefts haven't stopped. Since the box is in my office, I'm the most likely suspect."

"What kind of things are being stolen?"

"Power tools mostly. They're not worth that much on the street so it's hard to see why anyone would bother," Cheryl said. "But it costs us because when tools are missing, it screws up our schedules and of course, they are expensive to replace."

"If it weren't for the anonymous letters linking the thefts to the sexual harassment, I would never have thought the two things were connected," Larry said.

"Do you really think whoever sent the letters would hurt Tod?" I asked Cheryl.

Cheryl looked at Larry. He replied, "I've studied the letters, and I think we have to take the threats seriously."

"I can see Dennis running a scam," I said. "But I can't see him hurting a kid."

"How well do you know your brother?" Larry asked me.

I thought about it. Then I said, "I don't really know him. After his football injury, he changed into a man I don't know—a man who doesn't want anyone to know him."

"Then when you say your brother wouldn't hurt Tod, you can't be sure of that, can you?" Larry asked.

I hesitated. I thought about the sweet kid I had grown up with, and the angry, bitter man I had talked to not long ago. And then I said, "No, I can't be sure. I don't know my brother anymore. I don't know what he would do."

CHAPTER 14

I had to speak to Dennis.

Cheryl, Sally, and Larry talked on, discussing their ideas about Dennis and Barbara's scam, the thefts from Bauer's construction sites, and the threats against Tod.

All that was serious stuff, no doubt about it. But I only listened with one ear, because a terrible thought had entered my mind. As it grew inside me and I began to see a pattern to everything that had happened, I felt cold all over and I started to shiver.

Dennis, my brother Dennis, he was the key to everything. Dennis—with his harsh, angry eyes and his bitter words and his tight, grasping hands. Dennis . . .

Larry had been speaking, but he stopped suddenly and looked at me. "What's the matter, Janet. You're awfully quiet all of a sudden."

"I'm getting some ideas I don't like," I said.

132

"You look pale," Larry said. He came over to my chair and put his hand on my shoulder.

"I've felt better," I said. What would Larry and Sally say if I told them I needed to talk to Dennis? They would worry I was going to tip him off to our suspicions that he and his legal scam were behind everything that was going wrong. I could now see that so much of what Larry had done was designed to keep me from knowing he suspected Dennis. He must have suspected him for a long time. He had put me off because he didn't want to lie to me, but he couldn't tell me the truth either. He didn't want to put me in a position that trapped me in a conflict of loyalty between him and my brother.

It looked like now he had decided it was okay. He had believed me when I said I felt nothing for my brother and I had believed it too—until this very moment.

Why would Larry have been involved investigating Dennis's scam, prowling around Bauer's? Larry was a homicide cop. He didn't usually investigate petty thefts. I couldn't recall ever hearing him talk about investigating extortion either. And that's what it looked like Dennis and Barbara had going, an extortion plot to get money from men by accusing them of sexual harassment.

When had Larry's investigation caused him to stop seeing me? I thought back and realized Larry had been putting me off even before Barbara was killed.

Larry gently caressed my shoulder and my back. My muscles had tensed up. The picture that was forming in my mind was too terrible, it couldn't be true.

I forced myself to relax, to smile. "It's a lot to think about," I said. "We need to investigate more, see how it all fits together."

"I'm working on it," Larry said. "Do you have any ideas?"

"Yes," I said. "There's some things I want to check out."

"What?" Larry asked, looking at me uneasily.

"Uh, there's . . . Tod!" I said. "Yes, Tod. I think I need to talk to Tod."

"Leave him out of it," Cheryl said.

"Uh . . . you know those Nike clothes he wears? They're expensive. Gang kids rip them off. Some kids steal to get clothes like that."

"So?" Cheryl said. I could see she didn't like where I was going. And to tell the truth, I was just talking while my mind went racing off in a different direction. I wanted to put them all off the track and until the words popped out of my mouth, I hadn't given Tod's cool clothes a thought.

"Yes, Tod," I babbled on. "I'm going to talk to him. I'll get Porsha to come with me."

I grabbed my backpack and called to Lech. As I was going out the back door, I heard Larry's voice calling. "Janet? Where are you going? Janet? Hey, wait a minute . . ."

*   *   *

I ran out into the alley with Lech at my heels. I could hear the sound of heavy machinery ripping up the parking lot. As I came out onto the street I saw that the air was full of dust, small pebbles, and grit, which swirled around me, driven by the high wind.

I raced along the street, turning corners at random until I figured that if Sally or Larry had tried to follow me, I'd have lost them. Then I ducked into a doorway out of the wind, pulled out my cell phone, and called my brother.

His secretary said he was in a meeting. I told her I was his sister and it was an emergency.

"Dennis?" I said as soon as I heard his voice. "We've got to talk."

"What's the matter, why did you get me out of a meeting?" He sounded angry.

"I have to talk to you right away," I said. "It's serious and it can't wait."

"What are you mixed up in now?"

"It's what *you* are mixed up in," I said. "Where can we meet?"

"We aren't going to meet," Dennis replied. "I have nothing to say to you."

"I've been talking to Cheryl," I said. "I read Tiffany's diary. I'm putting it together. And I'm working with Larry."

"Cheryl? You've been talking to Cheryl Spears?" Dennis said.

Something in his voice sent chills up my spine. I clutched at the phone. The rising wind seemed to want to pull it out of my hand.

"Look, Janet," Dennis said, "I have appointments all day today. How about tomorrow?"

"No! It can't wait that long. We have to talk today."

A long silence. He was plotting something, I could feel it. "Where are you?" he asked.

"At the W.R.C. office," I replied. "I'm meeting with Cheryl and Larry here, but I should be done soon. How about sometime this afternoon?"

Again a silence. Then he said, "The only time I have free is between four and five. I have two appointments in Glencoe and I can squeeze you in then. There's a deli on Park Avenue near where I'll be. We could meet there."

"Fine. I'll be there," I said. "How do I get to the deli?"

"Take the train to Glencoe, get off there, and walk west

from the station on Park Avenue. You'll see the deli on the right-hand side of the street, about a half block west of Green Bay Road, okay?"

The train . . . if I took the train I'd have to leave Lech behind.

"Janet? Is that okay or not? I don't have all day."

"I'll see you at four," I said. I snapped the phone shut.

I stood there for a moment, thinking. Surely I could take the train. I wouldn't need Lech, I could trust my brother. But then I remembered that I'd thought someone was following me from Tiffany's, and again I felt the chill in my spine I'd experienced when Dennis said Cheryl's name. Better safe than sorry.

I checked my watch. Cheryl's lunch hour would be over, so she must be heading back to work now. But after what I'd said about Tod, maybe she'd want to talk to him.

I walked back toward the office. As I neared our corner, I saw Cheryl come out of the alley behind the W.R.C. and head west.

I followed.

She turned down Pitner. Just as I thought, she was going to the high school.

As we approached the school, I saw a bunch of kids standing just off the school grounds, smoking. Cheryl went up to them, said something, and they pointed north. Cheryl strode off in that direction, and Lech and I followed.

The wind roared behind us, flinging food wrappers and torn newspapers into the air.

Cheryl picked up the pace. She jogged easily along the sidewalk, moving in and out of the knots of schoolkids lounging around outside the school. Turning the corner on Church, she trotted across the street to the playing field.

Lech and I kept our distance. Cheryl went up to a

group of kids standing on the edge of the field. One of them was Tod.

Cheryl said something to Tod, who waved at his friends and then joined her. They walked off and I followed.

As I came up behind them, I heard Tod saying, "No way, no way, no way!"

"Tod! Cheryl!" I called out.

They both turned. I could see at once that they were angry—they had been arguing. Tod looked close to tears and Cheryl's face was tight, her eyes blazing.

"We need to talk," I said. "Let's go over there." I pointed to a small park at the end of the block and we walked toward it without speaking.

Cheryl and I sat down on a bench. Lech stood at our side and Tod squatted down next to the bench, looking up at Cheryl. "I wouldn't do anything to get you in trouble, Cher, you know that," he said.

Cheryl glared at him.

"How did you pay for the Nike shoes and the neat skateboard?" I asked him.

"Like, big deal! My friend, Rick, he loaned me a few bucks," Tod said.

"And how were you going to pay him back?" Cheryl asked.

"No problem," Tod said. "He's cool with it."

"Did you do something for him?" I asked, looking Tod right in the eye. "If you did, we need to know about it."

"How did you find out?" Tod said, sinking down onto the dirt.

"By investigating and thinking," I said.

"I was afraid something like this would happen," Tod said. "I warned him, I told him he'd get Cheryl in trouble.

He said no way. The guy who wanted the keys promised him no trouble."

"Tell us," I said.

Tod sighed. It sounded like the sigh of a kid who was relieved to get something off his chest. "I swore not to tell," he said.

"But you know you have to now, right?" I replied.

"Well, like . . ." Tod took off his cap, scratched his head, put the cap back on. "This friend of mine, Rick? He comes to me one day and says this guy offered him, like, three hundred bucks if he'd, like, talk me into ripping off Cheryl's keys one night when she was asleep. All's I had to do was, like, take the keys, give them to Rick, and Rick would get them back to me the next morning before Cheryl woke up."

"Oh, Tod," Cheryl said.

"I said no way if it would get you in trouble, Cher, but he said, like, no one would ever figure you were involved. And, like, I stood to clear two hundred bucks. And he swore nothing bad would happen and no one would find out."

"You believed that?" I asked.

Tod looked at his feet. "I had to believe it," he said. "Because Rick—people do what Rick says. I was scared not to."

Cheryl turned back to me. "Rick is someone Tod knew from when he was on the street. Rick is a scary guy." She turned to Tod, pulled off his cap, and ran her hand over his hair. Then she put his cap back on. "You shouldn't have done it," she said. "But I see where it looked like you had no choice and the bucks were good."

"I'm real sorry if you got into trouble over what I did," Tod said. "I went to the W.R.C. for help. I was afraid what was going on at work, at Bauer's, the trouble you were in? I was afraid it was because of, like, what Rick made me do. I felt so bad."

"You did right to tell Janet and me," Cheryl said to her brother. "You better get back to school now. Don't worry, it will be okay."

Tod took off, and Cheryl and I looked at each other.

"I'm surprised you aren't mad at him," I said.

Cheryl sighed. "He's only a kid," she said. "I just want him to talk to me and to trust me and to tell me when he's got troubles. Getting mad wouldn't do any good." She wrapped her arms around her chest and looked at me. "He's all I have and I'm all he has. We have to stick together. I can't let anything bad happen to Tod. He's been through enough."

"Does that mean you don't want Larry to know what he told us?" I asked.

"What do you think?" Cheryl replied. "Will Larry go after Tod? You know him better than I do."

"Rick is a street kid, right?" I asked.

"Right."

"Probably someone hired him to bully Tod and get your keys," I said.

"That's my guess too," Cheryl said.

"Rick and whoever he worked for used Tod. I don't see why Larry has to involve Tod. He can go after Rick and, hopefully, find out who hired him to get the keys. I believe Tod when he says he wasn't the one who stole stuff from the sites. And I'll tell Larry that."

Cheryl still looked doubtful. "Maybe I can figure a way to tell Larry about Rick without bringing Tod into it," she said.

As we spoke, we retraced our steps, turning on

Dempster and heading back to the W.R.C. office. "Don't you have to be back at work?" I asked Cheryl.

She looked at her watch, sighed, and quickened her pace. "I'm late, but I think we should get it over with—talking to Larry, I mean. When you ran out like that, he was upset, and he said he would wait for you to come back. I told him I was going to work, but of course, I really had to talk to Tod. After what you said, I wanted to get to him before you did." She sighed again. "I know where his friends hang out at lunch hour, so I figured I might find him before the end of the school day. And it worked. At least it wasn't Tod who was stealing stuff."

"You believe him too?"

"Yeah. I trust him."

The love between Cheryl and her brother was beautiful to me. I envied it. I thought of my brother, Dennis. I didn't trust him. I don't think he cared what happened to me anymore—not since his accident, anyway. When my marriage broke up, I was in sad shape, but Dennis didn't even bother to get in touch.

I thought of Tod coming into the W.R.C. Caught between the bully, Rick, and his sister's well-being, he had done his best. I couldn't see Dennis worrying for one minute about any trouble I might find myself in.

But despite the fact that he acted like he didn't care if I lived or died, deep down I still worried about him. More and more clues were pointing to my brother—pointing to him as at the center of everything. Hiring a street kid to steal keys, getting the kid to steal equipment to use as a lever against Cheryl—that sounded just like Dennis. My instincts all told me Larry was after him, and if Larry was after him, he had done something bad, something very bad.

Trust him? I didn't trust my brother one little bit.

But when we were small, when I was scared to walk down the street by myself, he would take my hand and walk with me and protect me. He had changed, that was true, but I still had those memories and they weren't going to go away.

My steps got slower and slower.

Cheryl was walking ahead of me now, heading toward the W.R.C. office.

Beyond her, I could see the yellow front-end loader. It lifted a huge shovelful of asphalt chunks, swung it over, and dumped it on top of the pile rising in front of our office.

Then it pivoted, and its backhoe end rose up. The long arm stretched out, then sank down and dug deep into the parking lot. It gouged out a chunk of asphalt.

The hoe rose up into the air. The cab started to turn and the long arm of the backhoe reached the top of its arc and began to descend.

Suddenly I started to run. "Cheryl!" I screamed, "Cheryl, watch out!" But in the noise of the wind and the roar of the machinery, she couldn't hear me. She strode along, her head high, looking forward, right under the arm of the backhoe.

"Cheryl!" The wind blew away my words, I could barely hear them.

I ran as fast as I could, under the backhoe arm, right at Cheryl, and gave her a terrific shove.

With all my strength, I butted her out onto the street between two parked cars.

As we stumbled over the curb, the backhoe tilted its bucket and out tumbled a stream of gigantic asphalt chunks, huge rocks, and gravel. It poured out onto the sidewalk where a moment before, Cheryl had stood.

Chunks tumbled onto the street, striking us and knocking us off our feet.

I lay on the street, dazed. I looked up to see Lech, standing over me, whimpering. He had been right by my side. He must have been hit too. I sat up slowly. Blood trickled down my cheek. My clothes were torn. A chunk of rock lay on top of one of my legs. I pushed it away and stood up shakily, checking myself over. I was cut and bleeding from scratches on my face and hands. But my body, protected by my jean jacket and jeans, was only bruised. I quickly checked Lech, smoothing my hands over him. He didn't flinch. He was fine.

"Janet? Are you okay?"

I turned to see Cheryl, sitting just behind me. Her face was bleeding too. Her jacket was torn and she was covered with mud and dirt.

"Nothing serious," I said. "How about you?"

"Bruised but no real harm done. What happened?"

"I don't know," I replied. "I was watching the backhoe and all of a sudden it looked like it was aiming to dump its load right on you. I tried to shove you out of the way. Looks like I didn't quite make it."

We both looked at the place where Cheryl had been a moment before.

A giant pile of jagged rock and stone and asphalt chunks lay there, bits still sliding from the top down onto the curb and the street.

A guy climbed out of the backhoe cab and walked over to us.

"Sorry about that, ladies, the thing just went haywire there. Don't know what happened." He gave a strange, ugly grin. "Better watch your step. Next time you might not be so lucky."

"That wasn't luck!" Cheryl said. "Janet saved my life!"

The man didn't answer. He turned and walked away.

"I don't get it," Cheryl said. "How come that guy isn't wearing a hard hat? Something weird is going on."

"Hey! Cheryl!" A man holding two coffee cups, wearing work clothes and a hard hat, came running up to us. "Who was that? What happened? Are you okay? Who was driving my backhoe?"

Cheryl said. "That guy? I never saw him before." She turned to me. "Bill here, he works for Mr. Bauer."

Bill said, "I was working the backhoe till about ten minutes ago. Then that man, the one you were just talking to, he comes along, says he works for Bauer, and wants to talk to me. Could I get out of the cab for a minute?"

"You know him?" Cheryl asked.

"I never saw him before in my life," Bill said. "But I thought, okay, maybe he's new or something. So I got out to talk to him like he wanted. And then he asked me to get us both coffee. And when I come back, he's working my backhoe, dumping a load on you guys. I couldn't believe my eyes. He almost killed you!"

We all turned to stare after the man who had been driving the backhoe—the man who had checked, seen we were okay, obviously been surprised and unhappy that we were, and calmly walked away.

We looked up and down the street, but the man had disappeared.

CHAPTER
15

As I approached the deli, I saw Dennis standing on the sidewalk, leaning on his cane, watching for me.

As I came up to him, he began walking toward me. "Let's go to the park by the lake and talk there," he said.

Despite his cane, he moved quickly and I had to take long strides to keep up. We crossed the tracks and walked east. Ahead of us, we could see the lake. The water was dark, almost black, and huge waves rushed onto the shore, foaming along the top. The sky was a dirty yellow-gray and glowed with an eerie yellow light. "That's a tornado sky," I said uneasily.

Dennis didn't reply. He swung his cane as he walked, so it made a swooshing sound. "Where's your dog?" he asked.

"You can't take a dog on the train," I replied.

"Right."

Park Avenue turns into a parking lot where it ends at the lake. Beyond the lot, a narrow lane curves off, down the bluff, toward the lake. Dennis walked toward it.

"Where are we going?" I said, glancing around. A car drove into the parking lot behind us and parked.

"Just shut up," Dennis snapped. "What you and I have to talk about has to be discussed in private."

We set off on the narrow road. It entered the trees and wound downward, and soon you could no longer see the lot or the park. We were among a stand of trees, their branches tossing wildly in the violent wind. Dennis looked around. I did too. There was no one to be seen. Dark shadows pooled under the trees.

Dennis stopped. "Okay, let's talk. What did you want to see me about? What's this about Cheryl Spears?"

"Here?" I said. "You want to talk here, in the middle of nowhere? There's not even anyplace to sit down."

"Just say what you have to say," Dennis said, looking at his watch, "I haven't got all day. I have an appointment at four."

"Dennis," I began, "I know we haven't been close for years—"

"That's an understatement," he said.

"But you're still my brother and I don't want anything bad to happen to you."

"Cut the crap," he said. "Just tell me what you have on your mind, okay?"

"They know what you're doing, the extortion racket you and Barbara had going!" I burst out. I had meant to lead up to it gradually, but his angry, twisted face brought out all my old teenage fear of my big brother and his temper. "They're going to get you. You have to stop."

"Who knows?"

"The W.R.C.—"

Dennis laughed. "Big deal."

"And Larry. He knows too."

"Larry!" Dennis spat out. "He's got no evidence."

"I don't think that's true. He was working with Barbara, and now he's tight with Cheryl."

"Yeah, that's where I went wrong. You do a deal with a man, he keeps his side of the bargain. You try and make a business deal with a woman, and she loses her nerve every time. It drives me crazy." He swung his stick angrily into the air. It made a whirring sound.

"You know that's not why they stopped working with you," I said.

"Barbara and I had a good thing going," Dennis said. "Through Sink, Barbara had connections with most of the employers in town. She knew where we could make a case, and she sweet-talked the women into going along. We were making money hand over fist. Then all of a sudden, she says she can't do it anymore."

"Were you and she—?" I said gently.

He twisted his cane in his hands. "For a while, but then everything started going wrong. Barbara kept nagging at me to drop the suits. She wanted to drop the suit against Sink. She said Sink never harassed her, not really. Then she said Tiffany wouldn't go along either because Tiffany decided she was in love. That did it, because Sink was the one I wanted to get most of all!" Dennis smacked his cane angrily on the ground. "Barbara was going to blow our entire operation!"

"What about Cheryl?" I asked.

"Cheryl! That fell apart too, because Barbara lost her

nerve. Barbara kept saying Cheryl was too loyal to Bauer, she'd never agree to sue him. I told Barbara she was wrong. I'd see to it that Cheryl went along, and Bauer would be good for hundreds of thousands. As for Sink, I knew he would settle. But Barbara said no, I had to drop the cases, or she'd go to Larry. She said that there were real, serious cases of harassment. Women losing their jobs, not getting promotions, and claims like ours created a backlash and made it harder for the true ones. True ones! What a laugh."

"So you and she disagreed?" I asked.

"Disagreed? Yes, you could put it like that." A sound caught his attention. "What was that? Did you hear it? Is there someone there?"

I looked around, but I didn't see anyone. Dennis darted back up the lane. To my surprise, he didn't use his cane when he ran.

A few seconds later he came back. "There's no one there, but I don't like this. Did you tell anyone we were meeting?"

"I thought you needed your cane to walk," I said.

"I can move just as fast without it, but I limp," Dennis said. "Besides," he swished the cane through the air, "it comes in handy."

He grabbed my hand and half led, half dragged me along the path. "Come on, let's go farther in. No one will see or hear us if we talk behind the sanitation plant down there."

I tried to pull my hand out of his grip, but he was incredibly strong. He pulled me along until we stood, concealed from view, behind an old, seemingly abandoned, concrete building.

"Why are you telling me all this, about your plot to

extort money from Sink and Bauer?" I asked.

"Why not?" Dennis said. "You're my sister. You're not going to tell anyone, right?" He smiled an ugly smile. "I know you. If there's one thing about you that's for sure, it's that you're loyal."

I tried to smile back, but I felt sick inside.

His face darkened. "I thought Barbara was loyal—that was where I went wrong. Taking chances on women, that's where I made my mistake." He stepped out from the shadow of the building and walked up to a tree. A long, dead branch extended out over the narrow sidewalk that went around the building. He swung his cane and struck the branch. It broke in two and a long, heavy piece fell to the ground.

"Wow," I said. "You sure are strong."

"Your arms get strong when your legs are weak. You have to compensate," Dennis said. "But to tell the truth, this is a special cane." He smiled. "It's weighted, so I can use it for—defense. Sometimes my work takes me into dangerous neighborhoods, you know? I've trained until I can use it as a weapon."

"Did you take Barbara out into the woods to talk to her about business, just like you're doing with me now?" I asked.

Dennis looked at me. "Well, surprise, surprise! Little sister has figured it out," he said. "I never would have predicted it, not in a million years. I'd planned for everything, but you being smart—now, that's a possibility that never crossed my mind." His eyes narrowed. "Larry, your friend—Larry, the cop—you tell him what you figured out?"

My stomach was churning and I felt nauseous. My own brother had become possessed. But it was not a demon from hell that overpowered him. It was anger and bitterness and resentment. He was so full of anger he seethed with it. He was like a teakettle just coming to the boil, quivering, little spurts of steam coming out, and in a moment he would boil over. But before that happened, I had to hear him say it, I had to know what he had done.

"Why, Dennis, why?" I cried out. "Why did you have to kill Barbara and Tiffany?"

"And Cheryl, don't forget Cheryl. As soon as you said you were talking to her, I knew she had to go. Sooner or later she'd tell you what she knew, and sooner or later her kid brother would confess how I'd gotten the keys and set up the thefts from the construction sites to blackmail her."

"Cheryl's not dead," I said.

Dennis looked surprised.

"I pushed her out of the way of the backhoe," I said, "but not before she told Larry and me everything."

Dennis smiled, but the smile looked fierce and threatening. "It doesn't matter. Next time I'll hire someone more competent, someone who can do the job," he said. "And without Barbara and Tiffany and Cheryl, and without the files, which I took right out from under your nose, it doesn't matter what you know or what Larry knows. There's no evidence. That's the good thing about being a lawyer. I know what it takes to make a case and get a conviction. And without them to testify, you've got nothing that will stand up in court."

But then he stopped smiling. "The problem, Janet, is you. You won't give up. You won't stop until you bring me down. Why? What have I done to you? Why wouldn't you leave it alone?"

I eyed the branch and looked at Dennis. I could see he'd made up his mind. He was working up to it. It wouldn't be much longer now.

Suddenly his eyes blazed and his anger erupted. "Nobody is going to get in my way!" he screamed. "Nobody! You try it, you're—" He swung his cane down with so much force I could hear it whipping through the air.

But I had seen him shift his weight the moment before he struck and I dodged.

"Lech! Here, Lech!" I screamed. Far in the distance I thought I heard my dog barking and a man shouting. I bent down, grabbed the branch, and swung at my brother.

He stumbled out of my way, then swung his cane. But I stepped aside and raised the branch. I meant to hit him, I would have hit him, but Dennis swung faster and his heavy stick knocked the branch out of my hands, grazed my shoulder, and I fell to the ground.

I could hear Lech's barks coming closer. Dennis raised his cane and looked around anxiously.

"Lech!" I screamed. The barking was nearer now.

The cane came down and just as it struck, I rolled away. The cane plunged into the muddy soil and stuck there. Dennis lost his balance and toppled over on his bad leg.

The rising wind boiled around us, full of flying debris. Suddenly it was dark, so dark I could barely see beyond where Dennis yanked at his cane, trying desperately to pull it out of the mud.

I staggered upright and grabbed the larger half of the broken branch. I knew I couldn't outrun him and his arms were incredibly strong. Where, oh, where was Lech? Where was . . . ?

Dennis, struggling to rise, pulled his cane from the mud and screamed something. But the wind was making so much noise I could not hear him. *A tornado,* I thought. *The tornado is here, right now, passing over us!*

Lech bounded into the clearing. "Get him, Lech! Get him! Attack!" I shouted. I could barely hear Lech's barking in the rising roar of the wind, but he moved so fast all I could see was a huge black blur. He launched himself upon Dennis just as Dennis got to his feet and raised his cane.

They went down together—Dennis trying to hit Lech with his cane, Lech's jaws closing on Dennis's neck.

"Lech!" I screamed. "Hold!" If he heard my command, Lech would not hurt Dennis. No matter how angry he was, Lech would obey me.

But Lech couldn't hear my command and all he knew was that I told him to attack. Around us was the sound of the lake. The waves, high and crashing against the shore, driven by the wind, and the rain that had suddenly started to fall made such a roaring, screaming noise that nothing else could be heard.

The wind knocked me flat.

Branches flew through the air and I lay on the damp ground, the breath knocked out of me, unable to move as the tornado whirled around me, the wind so strong I was pinned to the ground.

Then the sound began to lessen, the wind to quiet slightly, and finally I was able to struggle to my feet and look around.

"Janet!" Larry came hurtling into the clearing. "Janet!"

Lech stood over Dennis's prone body. He raised his head and looked at me and let out his death cry. Above the roaring wind, his howl rose and quivered in the air. Larry and I stared at each other.

I called Lech off and Larry ran to Dennis. He knelt

down, looked at the huddled shape, and leaned over to put his fingers on Dennis's neck. He was very still for a moment. Then he rose, turned to me, and shook his head. "I'm sorry, I'm so sorry," he said. "Your brother is gone."

Lech trotted over to me and stood by my side. I dropped to my knees and threw my arms around him. He was shaking and moaning. "It's not your fault, darling Lech," I said to him. "You couldn't hear me, you couldn't hear the hold command. You obeyed the attack command—it's not your fault." Tears poured down my cheeks and all around us, the wind roared and the sound of the waves filled the air.

CHAPTER 16

My brother was dead, and it was my fault.

I sat in Mrs. Gretzky's apartment with my friends around me, my feet up on a footstool and a blanket over me. I leaned back on the sofa while my friends gathered round, and we tried to make sense of it all.

Larry was there, of course. He sat next to me, holding my hand. From time to time he smoothed my hair and whispered comforting words into my ear. Lech sat next to the footstool, his head on my ankle.

Cheryl and Tod were there, and of course, Sally and Porsha.

Mrs. Gretzky had put out coffee and soft drinks and nibbles. There was Polish beer, but Mrs. Gretzky told me I had to have a schnapps, a Polish drink that—if you drink it down in one gulp the way she does—can blow the top of your head off. My glass sat at my side, untouched. I didn't have the heart for it.

The phone rang. Mrs. Gretzky answered, then said, "I'll see if she wants to talk." She turned to me and whispered, "It's Alderman Synko."

I reached for the phone. "Hello, Sink," I said.

"I'm sorry about Dennis," Sink said. He sounded very sorry and concerned too. "I can't believe what they're saying, that he killed Barbara and Tiffany and he was trying to kill you when Lech attacked him?"

"It's true," I said. "I can't believe it either."

"He wasn't always like that," Sink said. He sounded very sad. "I don't know what happened to him."

"He was very angry at everyone," I said.

"I'm so sorry, Janet," Sink repeated, "If there's anything I can do . . ."

"You can tell all the officials who are trying to close down the W.R.C. to back off," I said. "And tell Bauer to withdraw our eviction notice and repair our parking lot."

"I'll do that, Janet, glad to," Sink said. "By the way, you weren't planning on telling people about me and Tiffany, or that Barbara was running her and Dennis's extortion racket out of my office, were you?"

"When do you think you can call off all the people trying to shut us down?" I asked.

"Right away, right away, don't worry," Sink said.

"Then I guess I won't tell anybody about you and Tiff and Barbara," I said. "But I can't control what the police say."

"I'm sure Larry will listen to your advice," Sink said, his voice as charming as the man on TV who swears that no insurance sales representative will visit if you dial their 1-800 number.

"Okay, I'll try," I said. I told him good-bye and hung up.

"Sink wants us to hush everything up," I told my friends.

"Might as well," Cheryl said. "It's all over now."

I looked at Larry. I knew he felt bad that he and Lech had been so slow to catch up to Dennis and me.

We had driven out to Glencoe together, Larry, Lech, and I, in Larry's car. I wanted to believe my brother wouldn't harm me because I felt I owed it to him to tell him what I suspected and hear his side of the story before I told my thoughts to the police. But I didn't want to take a chance with a man I feared had already killed two women and tried to have a third killed. So I needed Lech and Larry nearby. They followed me to the deli, and they were in the car that drove into the parking lot behind Dennis and me. They came along behind us on the path. Larry planned to leave enough distance between them and me so Dennis wouldn't hear them following, but he wanted to be close enough to come to my aid if I called out.

Who would have suspected that, at the moment I needed them most, the tornado would strike? I knew Larry blamed himself for coming on the scene too late, while I could not forgive myself for siccing Lech on Dennis with the attack command instead of the hold command.

I sighed. "You and Tod are so lucky," I said to Cheryl. "Family who help one another, that's a precious thing."

Cheryl hugged Tod. "Yes, we are lucky," she said.

"Don't be so sad, Janet," Larry said.

"Why didn't I tell Lech to hold!" I burst out. "Why did I have to say 'attack'?"

"You weren't thinking straight," Sally said. "Dennis was coming at you with his killer cane and a tornado was blowing down on you. You can't expect to keep your head clear at a moment like that."

"You said 'attack,' because that was the only way it would work," Larry said.

"What do you mean?" I asked

"That cane of Dennis's, we examined it and now we know he used it to beat Barbara to death. After she was dead, he hit her again with the branch to leave the right kind of marks on the wound and to get blood on the branch. But the cane was reinforced and weighted. If he had hit Lech with it, he would have killed him and then he would have got you. You did what you had to do."

"But he hit Lech with it when he broke into Sink's office, when he came through the window," I said. "And Lech was just bruised."

"Lech must have been moving and just been grazed by the cane. Otherwise, it would have broken his back, easy," Larry said.

"I should have guessed it was Dennis that night at Sink's office," I said. "Because of his leg injury, he had worked to make his arms strong to compensate. That's how come he could pull himself up out of the window so easily."

"You couldn't have guessed. Don't be so hard on yourself," Larry said.

"And the way Tiffany acted, I bet even if she didn't look, she heard the uneven sound of his step, maybe his cane on the floor. She knew it was him but she didn't want to tell me."

"Probably Tiffany thought you wouldn't help her if it meant working against your own brother," Sally said. "But she was on the way to tell you everything at the end, and Dennis couldn't let that happen."

"You were after Dennis from the very beginning, weren't you?" I said to Larry.

"Barbara came to see me," Larry said. "She was afraid he would try to kill her. She said that he had changed, that he got so angry when she tried to break up their scam, she feared for her life. I told her I couldn't help her. Homicide cops investigate *after* the crime, not before. But she begged me to at least go see Cheryl, see if Dennis had threatened her, and warn her to watch out. Barbara knew Cheryl wouldn't trust her because she had been Dennis's partner. So I talked to some of the other guys on the force, found out about the investigation of the thefts at Bauer's, and used that as an excuse to poke around and talk to Cheryl. I did it as a favor to Barbara—she was so frightened."

"Why did all you guys, you cops, act like you thought Barbara and Tiffany's deaths were accidents? You must have suspected Dennis all along, right?" I asked.

"We did, but we had no proof," Larry said. "We figured if he thought he was safe, he might make a mistake. I couldn't tell you, Janet. He was your brother, after all. I was sure you would think it only fair to warn him."

"You were right," I said sadly. "As soon as I suspected him, that's just what I did."

"You weren't wearing a wire, like, to get his confession?" Tod asked.

I shook my head. "Larry wanted me to, but I refused. Dennis was my brother. I couldn't do that to him."

"So if he hadn't lost it, gone after you, he might still have got away with murder?" Porsha asked.

I looked out the window. The weather had changed. It was raining, a dark, steady, cold October rain. The eerie, yellow sky and gusty winds of tornado weather had gone and now we were heading into autumn. Across the street in the little park, the tornado wind had blown all the leaves off the trees, so the branches were as bare as if it were the middle of winter.

"My brother thought he had nothing to fear from me," I said. "When he realized he was wrong, rage took over. He destroyed himself. I only wish I hadn't been a part of it."

"You did what you had to do, you always do," Larry said. "It was incredibly brave, to face him down like that, to give him that last chance."

"I owed him a chance to do the right thing," I said. "He was family."

"He took the chance and used it to try to kill you," Porsha said.

"Yes, and I couldn't let him do that," I said sadly.

"I'll drink to that," Larry said. "To Janet's courage!"

"To Janet! To Janet!" everyone shouted, raising their drink glasses.

I slugged back my schnapps and just like I expected, it almost took my head off.